...A DREAM SHARED
AROUND THE WORLD...

milkshakefilms

www.**goal**the**movie**.com

Also available in the GOAL series;
novelizations written by Robert Rigby:

GOAL!
GOAL II: LIVING THE DREAM
GOAL omnibus edition
(contains Goal! and Goal II: Living the Dream)

GOAL.

GLORY DAYS

OFFICIAL GOAL NOVEL BY ROBERT RIGBY

CORGI BOOKS

GOAL: GLORY DAYS
A CORGI BOOK 978 0 552 55409 1

Published in Great Britain by Corgi Books,
an imprint of Random House Children's Books
A Random House Group Company

This edition published 2009

1 3 5 7 9 10 8 6 4 2

The Random House Group Limited supports the Forest Stewardship
Council (FSC), the leading international forest certification organization.
All our titles that are printed on Greenpeace-approved FSC-certified
paper carry the FSC logo. Our paper procurement policy can be found
at www.rbooks.co.uk/environment.

Corgi Books are published by Random House Children's Books,
61–63 Uxbridge Road, London W5 5SA

www.kidsatrandomhouse.co.uk
www.rbooks.co.uk

Addresses for companies within The Random House Group Limited can
be found at: www.randomhouse.co.uk/offices.htm

THE RANDOM HOUSE GROUP Limited Reg. No. 954009

A CIP catalogue record for this book is available from the British
Library.

Printed and bound in the UK by
CPI Bookmarque, Croydon, CR0 4TD

Author's note

Events at World Cup finals become a matter of historical record – football fans all around the world remember the best goals, the top goal-scorers and the most nail-biting matches, not to mention penalty shoot-outs. But the real World Cup finals in South Africa are yet to take place, the draw for the group matches has not even happened. And, as the saying goes, a week is a long time in football, so when you read this, some players may have changed clubs, while some nations mentioned in the text may not even make it to the finals. All the action described and the results of matches are therefore a product of my own imagination.

Robert Rigby (March, 2009)

Goal: Glory Days *is a work of fiction. In some cases true life figures appear but their actions and conversations are entirely fictitious. All other characters, and descriptions of events, are the products of the author's imagination and any resemblance to actual persons is entirely coincidental.*

ACKNOWLEDGEMENTS
BASED ON THE CHARACTERS CREATED IN
GOAL!: THE MOVIE AND GOAL II: LIVING THE DREAM

Goal I and II: Original story by Mike Jefferies & Adrian Butchart

Producers Mike Jefferies, Matt Barrelle & Mark Huffam

Executive Producers Lawrence Bender & Peter Hargitay (Goal I);
Lawrence Bender, Jeff Abberley,
Julia Blackman & Stuart Ford (Goal II)

Co-Producers Danny Stepper, Jo Burn (Goal I);
Danny Stepper, Jo Burn, Raquel De Los Reyes &
Henning Molfenter (Goal II)

Associate Producers Allen Hopkins, Stevie Hargitay,
Nicolas Gaultier & Jonathan Harris (Goal I);
Allen Hopkins, Stevie Hargitay, Nicolas Gaultier,
Steve McManaman & Jonathan Harris (Goal II)

Special Thanks to
FIFA
adidas
Newcastle United
FA Premier League

Prologue

Summer 2006

'*Pass!*' screamed Santiago. 'Now! Give it, *now!*'

Around half of the sixty-nine thousand crowd inside Berlin's Olympiastadion were yelling virtually the same words, while the other half looked to be holding their breath and fearing the worse.

The winger had done all the hard work, effortlessly rounding the full back, pulling the covering centre back out of position and racing on towards the dead-ball line. The pass was on; all that was needed was a simple pull back into the path of the onrushing striker. The move had textbook goal written all over it.

Santiago knew exactly where the ball should

be played. He pointed to the spot, yelling again, 'Pass it, now!'

But the winger didn't pass. This was the World Cup Final: a place in football history beckoned and he was going for glory. Head down, he ran on, drawing the centre back further and further out. At the last possible moment, he feinted to the right and then cut inside, attempting to wrong-foot the centre back so that he could shoot for goal. But the centre back was a wily and experienced campaigner. Deftly, he stuck out his right foot and cleanly took the ball from the winger, who stumbled on for a couple of strides and then crashed to the ground in a vain and fruitless attempt to win a penalty.

'No!' yelled Santiago.

'Oh no,' groaned half the crowd as the other half breathed a collective sigh of relief.

'A waste! A total waste!' shouted Santi angrily as he watched the centre back clear the ball and then turn back to the winger and wag his finger like he was telling off a naughty schoolboy.

'Er . . . Santi?'

Santiago turned and looked back. Roz was

standing in the open doorway, clutching an empty glass in both hands.

'Oh, sorry, babe,' said Santiago, leaping to his feet. 'Did I wake you?'

Roz smiled. 'Just a bit. D'you think you could turn the TV down a little? And maybe turn *you* down a little too?'

'Roz, I'm really sorry,' said Santiago, grabbing the TV remote from the sofa and turning down the volume. 'I get so frustrated just *watching* football – I want to be out there, playing.'

'Sounded as though you *were* playing. What's the score anyway?'

'One–one, Zizou scored with a penalty and then Materazzi equalized.'

Zizou, correctly known as Zinedine Zidane, had been, until very recently, Santiago's team-mate at Real Madrid, and was arguably France's and one of the world's greatest ever players. He had retired from club football at the end of the season and the World Cup Final against Italy was his last competitive match. Almost everyone who wasn't Italian wanted to see the great man celebrate one more victory. Added to the

Champions League success he had enjoyed with Santi and his Real team-mates, it would be a fitting end to a glorious career. But Zidane and France were not finding the Italians easy to beat. Far from it.

'Seems to have been going on for ages,' said Roz.

'We're in extra time,' Santiago said, glancing at the screen again as he heard the crowd cheer another French move which broke down on the rock-solid Italian defence.

'Are we?' said Roz, smiling. She sighed. 'You know, I really am sorry you've missed all this, Santi,' she added softly. 'I know how much playing in the World Cup finals would have meant to you.'

Santiago shrugged. 'It wasn't to be.' He was doing his very best to disguise his obvious disappointment. He should have been there in Germany, part of it all, the greatest celebration of world football. Many of his club-mates had been there: Ronaldo and Roberto Carlos for Brazil, Raúl and Casillas for Spain, David Beckham and Gavin Harris for England and, of course, Zidane for France. But Santi had played no part in the tournament. And it was hurting. 'I've another chance in four years' time,' he said, walking over to Roz. 'I just have to make sure I take it. And anyway, missing the World Cup meant I could be here with you.' He rested one hand on Roz's bulging stomach. 'Both of you.'

Roz was pregnant; the baby was due very soon, and for all his World Cup disappointment Santi was genuinely delighted that he would be there for the birth, particularly as just a few months earlier it had looked as though Santiago and Roz would have no future together at all.

Santi's first season at Real had brought glory and an amazing lifestyle. But with the good life had come pressures and temptations, which at times Santi had been unable to resist. Eventually it had proved too much for Roz and she had left Santi and returned to their home in Newcastle.

The separation had been painful for them both, but now they were back together and Santi was determined that nothing would ever separate them again. 'You should be resting,' he said.

Roz laughed. 'I *was* resting. I was sleeping

until you and Zizou decided to wake me.'

'Come and sit down and watch the rest of the match. It'll probably go to penalties. You know how exciting that is.'

'A bit too exciting for me,' said Roz with a shake of her head. 'I'll get another glass of water and go back up to bed. You watch the game.'

Santiago nodded. 'If you're sure.'

'I'm certain. Just try to be a bit quieter if you can.'

'No problem,' Santi said, turning away and going back to the sofa. 'I promise.'

Roz went into the kitchen, opened the fridge and took out some bottled mineral water. She had filled her glass and was returning the bottle to the fridge when she heard Santi shout again, even louder than before.

'No! I don't believe it!'

Roz put down her glass and hurried into the living room. 'What is it? What's wrong?'

Santi was staring at the TV screen. 'It's Zizou. He just head-butted Materazzi, he's being sent off!'

One

Christmas 2009

The large Christmas tree, elegantly trimmed in white and silver, stood in the entrance hall to the house, shining out like a welcoming beacon. Santiago held his three-year-old daughter in his arms and smiled as he saw the tree lights reflected in her big, brown eyes.

It was early evening, a time that Santi always looked forward to when he was at home. It was little Rosie's bedtime and Santi liked nothing more than the moments they shared as he read to her from a favourite storybook while she drifted off to sleep.

Over the Christmas period they had changed their routine slightly, pausing by the tree for a few minutes so that Rosie could take a lingering look at the lights and the glittering decorations. She was gazing now in wide-eyed wonder at the star on the very top of the tree. Santi squeezed her gently and silently told himself for the thousandth time that he was a very lucky man. Becoming a father had changed him, made him grow up and be grateful for everything the game of football had given him. More than anything, that meant his wonderful wife, Roz, and his beautiful daughter, Rosie.

The sounds of music, chatter and laughter, drifted out through the closed doors to the living room. Roz was in there with some of their closest friends, and once Rosie was asleep Santi would rejoin them. But at that moment, there was nowhere in the world he would rather have been than standing there, gazing at the tree with the sleepy three-year-old in his arms.

Life had changed so much in three short years, and all for the better, although it had seemed for a while that Santi's football career had been in freefall. After the World Cup heartache there had been a series of niggling but persistent injuries, which had restricted his appearances for Real Madrid and given him no chance to establish himself in the international arena.

And then a new coach had arrived at the Bernabéu Stadium, bringing in his own ideas, plans, playing systems and transfer targets. Suddenly Santi found himself on the fringes of the squad. He had finally been fully fit but getting even fewer first-team starts or substitute appearances.

It couldn't continue. Santiago realized that to kick-start his career he needed to move clubs. The rumours began to fly, with massive speculation and wild predictions in the press. Both the Milan clubs were said to be tracking the situation and considering bids. Then German giants Bayern Munich were believed to be interested. In England it was rumoured that Santi would join former Real team-mate Jonathan Woodgate at White Hart Lane and become part of the Tottenham Hotspur set up.

But none of these moves came to fruition; no club seemed prepared to match Real's valuation of Santiago or to take a risk on a player who had suffered a string of injuries. Everyone knew that Santiago Muñez was a world-class player, but the fear had persisted that he might be injury-prone.

And then, almost out of the blue, a definite offer came in – an offer that Real were ready to accept.

It was all down to Santi, who had been amazed to learn that the offer was from none other than his former club, Newcastle United.

The Magpies wanted Santiago back; they'd never really wanted him to leave. Roz had been ecstatic at the thought of a full-time return to her home town, but wisely she left the final decision to Santi. It was his career, the move had to be right for his football as well as for personal reasons. But Santi hadn't needed to think for long – it would be almost like going home for him too. Newcastle was the place where his whole adventure as a professional footballer had begun, the place where he'd played his very best football. He had quickly decided he was going back, back to St James' Park and back to the fanatical Newcastle supporters, known throughout the football world as the Toon Army.

And before Santi had even made his return appearance, a new variation of a famous football song had been echoing down from the Gallowgate stand.

'He's coming home, he's coming home, he's coming,
Santi's coming home . . .'

It had got even better for the returning hero and the Toon Army when, in his first match back in the Premiership, Santi grabbed two goals. And that had just been a taster of things to come because since then Santi had returned to his very best goal-scoring form.

And away from football, Santi and Roz had still had their lovely home just outside the city, close to their old friends Jamie and Lorraine and to Roz's mum, Carol. And they had ended all the doubts and worries about their future together by finally going through with their long-delayed wedding.

Santi smiled as he looked down at his

daughter and saw that she had fallen asleep on his shoulder. 'Yes, you're a very lucky man, Santiago Muñez,' he whispered.

He walked to the staircase and was just about to take the first step up when the double doors to the living room opened.

'Come on, Santi, you're needed for charades. Jamie and Lorraine are—'

Santiago turned back. 'Shhhh.'

Gavin Harris, Santi's great friend and former team-mate at both Newcastle and Real Madrid, stood in the open doorway. 'Sorry,' he said in an exaggerated whisper, pulling the doors shut behind him and tiptoeing over to the stairs like a pantomime villain. He looked down at the sleeping Rosie and grinned. 'She certainly is a beauty, mate. Lucky she takes after her mum instead of you.'

'Very funny,' said Santiago. 'Just don't wake her.'

Gavin shook his head. 'Wouldn't dream of it.' He glanced back at the closed doors and then spoke even more quietly. 'So tell me, what d'you think of Luisa? Really?'

'She's very nice.' It was Santi's turn to tease. 'Much too nice for you.'

Luisa was Gavin's new Spanish girlfriend, the latest in a very long line of girlfriends. He sighed wistfully. 'I think she could be the one.'

Gavin's reputation as a playboy footballer had been well-earned and would take a long time to live down. And he could see that Santiago needed a lot more convincing. 'Look, I know you've heard it before, but I mean it this time, honest.'

Santiago grinned. 'You're sure it's nothing to do with the fact that her dad just happens to be the owner of the football club you're managing?'

'No, nothing, nothing at all,' said Gavin, looking wounded at the very suggestion.

Gavin was still living and working in Spain, but his career as a top-flight footballer had continued for just one most season after Real's Champions League triumph. The club had decided to let him go. It was fair enough – age was against him, his body had taken a lot of hard knocks and he'd been at the very top for a lot longer than many strikers. But rather than gradually slip down the leagues like many aging pros, Gavin had another plan. He loved football, and despite his lifestyle he'd still found time to take his coaching badges. After a short spell out of the game he surprised everyone by becoming a player/manager, not with an English lower league club but with ambitious Spanish Segunda B outfit, Bardenas FC.

And he was making a good job of it. His team were well-placed in the league and still in the *Copa del Rey*, the Spanish equivalent of the FA Cup, and Gavin was continuing to make his mark on the pitch with some spectacular cameo appearances as a super-substitute.

Over the Christmas break he'd returned to England to visit his friends, to set up some TV work and to take the opportunity to watch Santi play in the Boxing Day fixture against north-eastern rivals, Sunderland, over at the Stadium of Light. The match had been hard fought, a typical derby encounter, and had ended in a one–one draw.

'You played well yesterday, mate,' Gavin said. 'Carry on like that and you'll make the World Cup, no problem.'

'The squad, maybe,' said Santiago as Rosie shifted slightly in his arms. 'But there are a couple of strikers well ahead of me as far as making the team is concerned.'

Gavin shrugged his shoulders. 'All you can do is keep on keeping on, you'll make it. You have to, because I'll be out there working for TV and I'm not going all the way to South Africa without my mate Muñez.'

Two

Santiago received and controlled the pass without breaking his stride. He avoided a sliding tackle and struck the ball with awesome power from five yards outside the box. It screamed towards the goal, rising all the time, cannoned against the crossbar and rocketed upwards before bouncing back into play.

The Toon Army gasped in frustration and then, almost as one, burst into spontaneous applause. Santiago's name echoed down from the Gallowgate and rang around St James'; it was good to be playing again.

Christmas is a difficult time for Premiership footballers. Celebrations have to be muted because of the demands of matches, which come thick and fast over a short period.

The Magpies were facing Manchester City just three days after their Boxing Day fixture against Sunderland. They were leading by a goal to nil, set up by Santi who was really turning it on. He always wanted to play well, but today there was an added reason to impress. His mother, Rosa-Maria, and his fifteen-year-old half-brother, Enrique, had arrived that day from Madrid and were watching from up in the stands.

Rain was bucketing down and the wind was swirling on a dismal, English winter's day, not the greatest welcome for Rosa-Maria and Enrique. Playing conditions were atrocious, but Santiago was looking to sign off the match in style as it went into the final few minutes – if he got a chance.

Suddenly the chance came and unsurprisingly it was down to the conditions. A crossfield pass bounced once and then stopped dead in the mud. Santiago was closest to the stationary ball. There was no one up with him, so his options were to make for one of the corners and wait for reinforcements to arrive, play a backward pass, or go for goal. It was an easy choice.

He set off on a run, pushing the ball further forward than usual with each touch because it could easily have stuck in the mud again. He reached similar territory as he was in for his previous goal attempt, but this time, when he struck the shot, there was never a moment's doubt as to where the ball would finish up. The first attempt had been like a range-finder; this one screamed into the net, giving Joe Hart in the City goal absolutely no chance at all.

The crowd erupted as Santi set off on a mazy celebration run, pointing up to his mother and brother and shouting, 'That one's for you. For you!'

Enrique, like his half-brother, was a gifted footballer, but unlike Santi he was a midfielder. Santi had spotted and nurtured the youngster's talent back in Madrid, and after moving to Newcastle he had arranged for Enrique to come over for trials with the Magpies' academy.

Enrique had impressed and been offered a place with the Under Sixteen squad.

Now he was in England to take up the place. But there are strict FA rules about young players living within the club's local area, so the move meant Enrique would be living with Santiago and Roz and continuing his schooling in the UK. Santiago was delighted. After all, Enrique was family, and Santi wanted his half-brother to get every footballing opportunity he himself had been denied as a youngster. But he knew that Roz had some reservations about a fifteen-year-old moving in with them, family or not.

Rosa-Maria was staying with them for just one full day and then overnight, so she was anxious to spend as much time as possible with her much-loved granddaughter, Rosie.

'She's so beautiful,' Rosa-Maria said in Spanish. They were back from the match and Rosie was perched on her grandmother's knee. 'And every time I see her she gets bigger.'

'That's what babies do, Mama,' Enrique said, also in Spanish. 'They grow.'

Santiago smiled while Rosa-Maria just

shrugged – she was used to her son's sarcasm – but Roz, whose Spanish was very limited, had no idea what was being said. And she didn't like it.

'You'll have to speak English now you're living here, Enrique,' she said, a little more sharply than she intended.

Enrique stared at her. 'I was speaking Spanish for my mother,' he said in perfect English. 'Her English is not as good as mine. And don't worry, I'll make sure you know exactly what I'm saying.'

There was an awkward silence for a few moments; no one was quite certain what to say and Santiago decided the best idea was to change the subject. 'So what did you think of me today, little brother?' he said to Enrique. 'Not bad, eh?'

Enrique shrugged. 'Not bad – you missed a couple of good chances. You won't play in the World Cup if you keep missing chances.'

The World Cup. It was on the minds of everyone in football. The draw for the group stages at the finals had been made earlier in the month and with 2009 about to move into 2010, the great tournament seemed very much closer.

'Thanks a lot, little bro,' said Santi with a sigh.

Santi's journey to international football had been as rocky as the road to club success, and as complicated. When the international call first came, it came as expected from Mexico, the country of Santiago's birth and of his late father's birth.

But Santi had never actually *played* for Mexico, and after the 2006 World Cup he'd received another call – from Spain, the country of his mother's birth and the country where he was, at the time, plying his trade for Real Madrid.

It was a big decision, and one Santi felt he couldn't and shouldn't make alone. A family summit was arranged. Santi's Mexican grandmother, Mercedes, and his brother, Julio, flew in from their home in Los Angeles. And from the other side of Madrid, Rosa-Maria and Enrique made the considerably shorter journey.

The family sat down together over a meal and everyone had their say. But there was little argument. Santi instinctively felt he wanted to play for Spain and no one disagreed.

'Why should you choose Mexico?' said his

grandmother, Mercedes, as blunt and down to earth as ever. 'Your father took us across the border to America when you were just ten years old. All you ever knew in Mexico was poverty.'

So Santiago chose Spain. He played in a couple of friendly matches and notched his first international goal. But then the succession of injuries began and Santi quickly slipped from the international radar. By the time Euro 2008 came around he hadn't even made it back to the squad. And Spain, inspired by world-class front men Fernando Torres and David Villa, became European Champions in spectacular style.

Now, just days from World Cup year, Santi had made it back into the squad and had played his part in the later stages of qualification, albeit mainly as a substitute.

But Enrique was right. If Santi was going to make it into the World Cup starting line-up he had to take his chances and make it difficult for the Spanish manager to leave him out – and he also had to stay injury-free.

Three

Santiago was reading to Rosie who was tucked up in bed. Roz was in the kitchen preparing dinner, and Rosa-Maria and Enrique were sitting a little self-consciously in the living room. Waiting.

Rosa-Maria smiled at her son. 'It will get easier; you'll feel more comfortable. At home.'

'It'll be just like home if Roz keeps giving me orders,' said Enrique with a scowl.

'*Enrique!* They're giving you a wonderful opportunity. This is their home, you have to fit in and live by their rules.'

'*Rules!* It's always rules. I thought I could escape rules when I got away from Spain.'

'Enrique . . .'

Rosa-Maria fell silent as she heard footsteps coming down the stairs. The door opened and Santiago came in.

'Everything OK?' he asked, noticing another awkward silence.

His mother smiled. 'Fine. Is Rosie asleep?'

'Yeah. I didn't even get to finish the story.'

Rosa-Maria went to stand up.

'No, you stay there,' Santi said. 'Relax. I'll go help Roz with the meal.'

'I wanted to help,' Rosa-Maria said. 'She wouldn't let me.'

'Of course not,' Santi said. 'You're our guests. Relax, take it easy. You don't have to do a thing.' He smiled and went off to the kitchen, pulling the doors closed as he left.

Enrique grinned at his mother. 'You see, Mama,' he said. 'We don't have to do a thing. Not even obey any rules.'

Roz was the first to admit she wasn't the greatest of cooks. But she was a lot better than Santiago, so when they were entertaining she usually got to do the cooking. And she wanted tonight's meal to go particularly well because she had an announcement of her own to make.

The problem was, the meal was *not* going well. Roz had thought she was playing it safe: roast beef, roast potatoes, Yorkshire pudding, vegetables – a typical English meal. What could go wrong with a roast dinner? You just stuck it in the oven and waited.

But Roz had discovered that plenty could – and had gone wrong. The beef was overcooked and as tough as old football boots, the Yorkshire puddings were as flat as pancakes and the roast potatoes were burnt. Even the gravy had lumps in it.

Santiago was saying all the right things; it was 'delicious', and 'his favourite'. But Roz could see the looks that Rosa-Maria and Enrique were exchanging, and the way they were pushing the food around their plates rather than eating very much of it.

'You don't have to finish it,' Roz said as she saw Rosa-Maria slide a piece of beef under some overboiled cabbage.

'It's very nice,' Rosa-Maria said quickly. 'But so much, I don't usually eat so much.'

Roz didn't like to say that Rosa-Maria had hardly eaten a thing. 'I should have done something more Spanish,' she said. 'A paella, maybe.'

Enrique rolled his eyes and sighed.

'What?' said Roz defensively.

'Just because we're Spanish doesn't mean to say we eat paella all the time. You're English but I don't expect you to be eating fish and chips every meal.'

'*Enrique!*' Rosa-Maria snapped. 'Don't be rude. Apologize to Roz.'

'No,' said Roz quickly. 'No, he's right. It was a stupid thing to say. I just . . . I just wanted tonight's meal to go well.'

'It is!' said Santiago and his mother at the same time.

They looked at each other and then at Roz. She was smiling. 'It's a total disaster.'

Rosa-Maria didn't understand. She turned to Enrique for an explanation.

'*El desastre,*' he said.

Rosa-Maria turned back to Roz and shrugged her shoulders sympathetically as if to say, it wasn't *quite* that bad.

But it was, and Roz knew it. They all knew it. Roz started to laugh and then suddenly they were all laughing, even Enrique.

'I could make a sandwich,' said Roz, pushing her plate away. 'Or there's a pizza in the fridge.'

'Pizza!' said Enrique, delighted that he wouldn't have to wrestle with any more of the overcooked beef. 'I love pizza!'

Santiago sighed, relieved that the frosty atmosphere had at last thawed and that everyone finally seemed to have relaxed. 'Don't worry, Mama,' he said to Rosa-Maria. 'Roz will be here every day to look after Enrique and make sure he doesn't go hungry.'

Roz stopped laughing; it was time to deliver her news. 'Actually, Santi, I won't.'

The room went silent and everyone looked at Roz. She had to continue. 'I was waiting for the right time to tell you all, and I guess it's now. I'm . . . I'm going back to work.'

For a moment there was a stunned silence and then Santi spoke. 'Work? But—'

'At the hospital,' Roz said quickly. 'You know nurses are always in demand. It's a really good job in the intensive care ward – exactly what I've trained for.'

Rosa-Maria looked at Santi and then back at Roz. 'But what about Rosie?'

Roz knew that this was going to be the difficult bit. 'Oh, it's fine,' she said. 'Everything is arranged.'

Four

'Why didn't you say something before? You made me look stupid in front of my mother too.'

Santiago was angry and so was Roz. They were arguing, but trying to do it quietly for fear of waking everyone else in the house.

'Oh, and we couldn't have that, could we?' hissed Roz. 'There's no way Santiago can be embarrassed in front of his mama! And I *did* tell you I was looking for a job again – you just didn't *listen*!'

The remainder of the evening had gone badly. Rosa-Maria went off to bed as early as possible, making the excuse that she had to be up early for her flight back to Madrid the following day.

Enrique slunk off to his room soon after.

'There's no need to be sarcastic, Roz.' Santi was trying to stay calm. 'You should have told me about the job – *made* me listen. And you definitely didn't say you'd been for an interview.'

'I didn't think I'd get the job,' said Roz defensively. 'And anyway, you'd have tried to talk me out of it. You've never wanted me to go back to work.'

'We've hardly ever talked about it.'

'Because every time I start to talk about it you change the subject. Santi, I've always said I'd wanted to go back to work at some stage.'

'At some stage, yeah, but Rosie is only three years old.'

Roz was struggling to keep her voice down. 'And that's old enough! And it's not that she's going to a stranger – Lorraine's my best friend as well as being a registered childminder. Rosie's known her all her life. It's perfect.'

Santi slumped down onto a sofa. 'Got it all sorted out, haven't you, Roz.' Roz didn't reply and Santiago looked at up her. 'It's not as though we need the money.'

'Oh, Santi,' said Roz, coming to sit next to him. 'Don't you realize that it's not about money? I love nursing, I always have. I love nursing like you love football. And I've spent years studying for this; it's a promotion and it's important to me.'

For a few moments, neither of them spoke. Deep down, Santi knew he was being unreasonable and that Roz had just as much right as he did to pursue the career she loved.

But he was still unsure how it would all work. 'What about Enrique? How's he going to get to the academy, and school?'

'Like millions of other kids,' answered Roz. 'On the bus. Santi, it was your idea that he came here. I wasn't sure about it but I agreed. But there's no way I'm going to be his taxi driver – he has to get on and do things for himself.'

'But this is all new to him. It's a lot to cope with.'

'And we'll help him, both of us. But you can't leave it all to me, Santi, that's not fair. Look, I'm married to a footballer but that doesn't mean to say I'll ever be like one of those TV footballers' wives. Or a WAG.'

Santi laughed. 'I know that. And I'm glad.'

'Good.' Roz glanced at her watch. 'It's getting late. We'd better get some sleep if we're going to get your mum to the airport on time in the morning.'

She went to get up, but Santi took her hand. 'I'm sorry, Roz,' he said. 'I shouldn't have got angry.'

Roz smiled. 'And I'm sorry too. I should have told you about the interview.' She leaned over and kissed Santi. 'Come on, let's go,' she said as she got up and walked over to the door. 'Otherwise your mama will tell me off for keeping you up too late.'

'Yeah, ha ha,' said Santi. 'Roz?'

Roz looked back. 'Yes?'

'Congratulations. I'm proud of you.'

Five

A biting wind shivered its way in from the north-east coast. Santiago, huddled into his thick overcoat, stood on the touchline of one of the many pitches at the Newcastle training complex. It was a bitterly cold winter's evening and Santi was the only spectator at a practice match being enthusiastically played by members of the academy's under-16s outfit.

Santi was smiling, and not just because his brother was putting in a confident and impressive performance in his first match of any sort with the squad. Santi was enjoying the football, despite the cold, but he was also thinking back to his own very first appearance at the complex.

He had just arrived from Los Angeles, a complete unknown, walking out in borrowed boots to join a practice match between teams made up of first-team regulars and reserves. It had been pouring with rain, cold, bleak, windy, totally different to the Los Angeles sunshine that Santi was accustomed to. And it had been tough, a real baptism of fire, particularly as a hard man, a veteran defender by the name of Hughie Magowan, had taken it on himself to give Santi a special north-eastern welcome by clattering him to the ground at every possible opportunity.

Santi had put in a pretty ordinary performance and his first appearance at the training complex had almost been his last. But he had stuck at it, eventually convincing the manager at the time that he was worth his place at the club.

Out on the pitch, Enrique was growing in confidence by the minute and was starting to boss the midfield area. He intercepted a ball in his own half, advanced fifteen yards, all the time gesturing to his fellow midfielders and forwards where he wanted them to run, and then deceived the opposition defence with a delightful chipped ball to one of his strikers.

Santiago smiled and nodded his appreciation. It was a terrific start, and it needed to be, because compared to most of the young hopefuls, Enrique had very little time to make his mark at the academy. Many of them had been part of the academy system for years, being guided, nurtured, encouraged, monitored and constantly assessed. Some had not made it this far, but at the age of fifteen everyone who remained knew he was rapidly approaching a major milestone in the bid to become a professional footballer.

Until now, they had all been on schoolboy forms, training a couple of evenings and Saturdays each week and playing matches on Sundays against other academy teams.

But soon, at the age of sixteen, each boy would learn whether or not the club wanted him to stay on and join its Youth Training Scheme – in effect, a footballing scholarship, which can last for up to three years. During that time, if retained each year, the young players would progress through the youth teams to the reserves.

If they were lucky, and extremely talented, they could be offered professional terms from the age of seventeen onwards, but most would have to wait until they were nineteen before finding out if they would have a longer-term future at the club.

Out on the pitch, the academy coach refereeing the practice match blew his whistle and Enrique, running with the ball, came to a standstill. He turned back and glared at the coach who was indicating that he had committed a foul.

'But I played the ball!'

Santi heard the shout from the touchline. He shook his head and sighed. There was no doubting his brother's passion and enthusiasm for the game.

'Don't argue with me, son,' the coach said. 'It was a foul. Now get on with it.'

Enrique nodded and backed away from the ball so that the free kick could be taken.

This time Santiago was not smiling. He knew from experience that his half-brother had a temper with a short fuse, not the best attribute on a football pitch. Enrique's birthday was in the summer; he had just six months to convince the club he was worth keeping on, and temper tantrums wouldn't help his cause. If he did make it he would continue his education at a local college as well as do jobs around the club.

But even if he did clear that next huge hurdle, there were still no guarantees. Very few kids make it all the way to full Premiership professional. Sometimes the early promise fades: a youngster who looks like a world-beater at ten or eleven may be little better than his schoolmates by the time he reaches fourteen. Some kids, a few, find the desire to make it as a pro diminishes as they grow older, while others realize before they are told that they are never, after all, going to be as good as they dreamed. A few suffer an injury that prevents them continuing, and some never reach Premiership standards but move into the lower leagues or even abroad to continue a career.

At Newcastle, the great Paul Gascoigne made his debut for the first team just months after leading the youth team to FA Youth Cup glory.

But players like Gazza and Wayne Rooney, who turned pro with Everton at seventeen, are exceptions, and exceptional talents.

Even the legendary Manchester United youth squad of the early Nineties, which featured stars of the future like David Beckham, Ryan Giggs, Paul Scholes, Nicky Butt and the Neville brothers, included others who never made it through to the big time.

Everything had been explained in great detail to Enrique, his mother, and to Santi. And Santi had stressed time and time again to his young brother that he could only succeed by putting in every ounce of effort over the coming months.

The whistle for the end of the session sounded and Enrique came trotting over to his big brother.

'How did I play?'

'Good, but you shouldn't argue with the ref.'

'But it wasn't a foul,' Enrique snapped, his temper flaring again.

'Enrique! You're here to learn. To listen, to watch, and to learn. The guys you're working with have been in football all their lives, they live it and breathe it. They know every move, every kick, every tackle, every tactic and every foul. They've done it all and they've seen it all. So don't think you know better than they do because you don't, and you probably never will.'

Enrique was breathing heavily but he nodded his acknowledgement that Santi was right. They walked back towards the changing rooms.

'While I was watching I was thinking about when I first arrived here,' said Santiago.

'Is this one of those "Back in the Day" stories?' said Enrique with a sigh. 'Because I'm cold and I need a shower.'

'It is an old story,' said Santi. 'But maybe one you should hear. I want to tell you about Jamie.'

'Jamie?'

'Jamie Drew, you've met him at the house. The guy married to Lorraine, who looks after Rosie.'

'Oh, yeah,' said Enrique. 'Your friend, Jamie. The plumber.'

Santi smiled. 'That's him. But he wasn't always a plumber. When I arrived here, he was in the reserves too. And he was good, really good, a midfielder. Watching you reminds me of Jamie – you play similar games.'

Enrique looked at his brother. 'I didn't know. He doesn't talk about being a footballer.'

'No, he doesn't talk about it.'

'Because he wasn't quite good enough?'

'He could have been one of the best.'

Enrique looked confused. 'So what happened?'

'It was the day of my first game for the first team. I came on as sub; we were playing at Fulham. Jamie played for the reserves.' Santi paused for a moment, remembering the mixed emotions of the day. 'Jamie told me later it was just a tackle, a hard tackle; he twisted his leg as he went down. He was in hospital when I got back from London. The knee was shattered and the lateral cruciate ligament was ruptured. Jamie never played again.'

They were almost back at the changing rooms.

'Why are you telling me this now?' said Enrique.

Santiago shrugged his shoulders. 'Maybe to remind you how lucky you are to be here. And no matter how good you are, Enrique, there's a lot of stuff that can happen to stop you making it all the way.'

'I know that,' said Enrique, 'and I'm sorry about Jamie.' His eyes hardened. 'But I'll make it, Santi. I'll make it.'

Six

Roz was careful to stick to the speed limits as she drove from one side of the city to the other. She was always a cautious driver, but even more cautious when she had little Rosie strapped into the child seat in the rear of the car. She was in a hurry, but that didn't mean she was going to put Rosie or herself in any danger.

Santi was off with the team on an away match and Roz had received a text from Enrique saying he'd forgotten his house key. He was waiting outside and it was raining, hard.

'If he's got any sense he'll wait in the outhouse in the garden,' said Roz to herself more than to Rosie, who wasn't listening anyway but staring out at the rain and the passing traffic.

Roz was glad to be back at work, back on the wards, doing something really useful. She didn't go into nursing to get rich – that didn't happen – but being married to a top Premiership footballer made it possible to live a very rich lifestyle, so it felt more important than ever to do something worthwhile with her life.

And it was going well; Roz's bosses were doing everything they could to help make her return as smooth as possible. The job was four days a week, and part of the back-to-work package was that it was mainly day shifts with only occasional nights, which helped a lot.

But even on day shifts, nursing isn't a nine-to-five job and there were often emergency situations to be dealt with, meaning that Roz often had to call Lorraine to let her know she was going to be late picking up Rosie.

Today was one of those days. Roz had only just collected Rosie and was trying to get home quickly. But it was rush hour; the city roads were jam-packed and the rain was delaying progress even more.

Roz joined a line of cars queuing at a busy roundabout and smiled as she heard Rosie start to sing a song she'd picked up from the radio. The car finally reached the front of the queue and Roz wiped a hand across her side window, which was steaming up slightly.

There was a gap in the approaching traffic and Roz pulled out. Suddenly, a car came hurtling out of nowhere, going much too fast. Roz instinctively stood on the brakes. There was a screech of more brakes from behind and then a thud as the vehicle following crunched into Roz's.

Enrique wasn't in the garden outhouse. He'd found the side door of the large double garage unlocked and was in there, playing keepy-uppy with a football. He was good at it; both feet, head, even his shoulders. He could hold the ball on an instep and then flick it up and make it come to rest on the back of his neck between his shoulders, just like some of the great ball players he'd seen at the Bernabéu.

But even keepy-uppy gets boring after a while.

He flicked the ball upwards and as it came down he hit a perfect half volley that clanged into the garage doors and bounced away.

Enrique sighed. He was missing home, his parents, his friends, Madrid. Santi and Roz were nice enough, and good to him, but they were both busy and rarely had much time to talk. The academy was going really well, at least Enrique thought it was; the coaches had been very enthusiastic about his attitude and progress.

The other bonus was little Rosie – she'd taken a real shine to Enrique, who she called 'Reekay'. And surprisingly, 'Reekay' felt the same way about Rosie. She was a delightful little kid, and although Enrique was technically her uncle, he felt she was more like the little sister he'd never had.

Life in England was good, like his mother said it would be, except for one thing – school.

It wasn't the lessons or the change from learning in Spanish to English. That was difficult, but Enrique's English was good and getting better all the time. It wasn't the teachers, most were great as were the majority of the other kids. After all, it was no longer unusual for kids from other European countries to be at British schools and Enrique was by no means the only newcomer to England in his year group.

The problem was very specific: three boys of Enrique's age who had decided they didn't like him and were ganging up to make his school life as miserable as they could.

Enrique went to the open side door, leaned against the frame and stared out at the rain, deciding that it was probably his own fault. He'd gone into the school trying to impress at first, boasting about how he was at the academy and that his big brother was the famous Santiago Muñez.

He hadn't meant to do it – it had just been nerves – but once he'd started boasting it was almost as though he couldn't stop, for a few days at least. He'd boasted about how he'd run wild in Madrid and even about hotwiring his brother's Lamborghini sports car and driving it away from a nightclub when Santi was inside. He didn't tell them though that he'd crashed the car and ended up in hospital. He just wanted to sound big, important and by the time he realized he was getting it completely wrong, it was too late: the ringleader, Jake Hodge, and his two mates, Jordan Cole and Craig Cameron, were on his case. Big time. And Enrique had been bullied before, in Spain – he knew the signs and knew he could be in for a rough time.

Enrique sighed. '*Stupido*.'

Then he heard a car. It didn't sound like Roz's VW; this vehicle arrived with a throaty growl, sounding more like a sports car of some kind.

He went round to the front of the garage and saw that it was, after all, Roz's car. She had driven it close to the house and Enrique spotted instantly what was causing the noise. The exhaust pipe was hanging loose and the back bumper and hatchback door were badly dented.

Roz switched off the engine and got out just as Enrique approached. 'I'm sorry,' she said quickly, as if worried that Enrique was going to launch into a complaint about waiting out in the rain for so long.

But he didn't.

'For what?' he said.

'For . . . for being so late back.'

Enrique shrugged. 'It doesn't matter. Are you OK?' He looked pointedly at the car.

'Yeah,' said Roz, nodding gratefully. 'It looks worse than it is, really. But it was a shock.'

'And, Rosie, is she . . . ?'

'Reekay!'

Enrique looked into the rear of the vehicle and saw Rosie in her seat with both arms stretched out towards him. He smiled, opened the car door and released her from the safety seat. He lifted Rosie from the vehicle and she clung to him with both arms around his neck.

'Let's get inside,' said Roz. 'It's been quite a day.'

They walked towards the front door and Roz fished her house keys from her bag.

'Have you told Santi about the accident yet?' asked Enrique as they reached the front door.

Roz shook her head. 'Not yet. I don't want to worry him before a game, and it was only a bit of a shunt after all. I'll tell him later, after the match.' She slid her key into the lock. 'Anyway, how was your day? Apart from losing your door key, that is.'

Enrique smiled. 'Good. Really good.'

Seven

Newcastle United was a club in crisis. After the traumas and uncertainties of recent seasons, a spate of injuries was the last thing the club needed, but as the winter moved on it seemed there were more first-team squad players on the treatment tables than there were fit to make it onto the pitch. It was the worst injury situation anyone could remember and had been getting worse since the beginning of the season. Some early injuries cleared up quickly but others lingered or were long-term and the squad had been steadily weakened and thinned.

The manager brought in new players during the January transfer window, but suffered a further blow when two of the new additions were crocked within their first couple of games.

Doom-mongers began talking about a jinx while more sensible heads knew only too well that it was a run of bad luck that could hit any club at any time. But that didn't make it any easier to cope with.

Fortunately for Santi he'd remained injury-free, but the situation meant that extra responsibility fell on the shoulders of him and the other fully fit senior players. The young reserves and the newcomers had to be nursed and shepherded into the rigours of the Premiership, which many football observers reckoned was not only the best but also the toughest league in the world.

It wasn't the ideal time to be facing Chelsea at Stamford Bridge, especially as they were riding high in the Premiership and fighting hard for the title under the guidance of Luiz Felipe Scolari, or Big Phil as the press liked to call him.

And as Santi took his position for the kick-off he couldn't help but acknowledge that, whilst almost every member of the Chelsea team were full internationals and household names, many of the Newcastle players would be very largely unknown to anyone outside Newcastle.

Chelsea, organized and experienced, began the match full of movement and ideas, with Frank Lampard and the little Portuguese maestro, Deco, pulling the strings and orchestrating many of their early attacks.

Newcastle were stretched but holding on and restricted to the occasional counter-attack, which mostly foundered on the rocks in Chelsea's defence, John Terry and Ricardo Carvalho.

Joe Cole went close for Chelsea, driving in a shot from twenty yards out, which Shay Given, excellent as always, did well to turn round the post.

Santi was playing deeper than he would have liked, protecting his midfield from the surging runs of Deco and Cole through the middle, and full back Ashley Cole down the flanks.

But close to the end of the first period and totally out of the blue, Newcastle found themselves one up, courtesy of Santiago Muñez.

Collecting the ball ten yards inside the Chelsea

half he set off on a rampaging run, with a change of pace that left the opposition defenders floundering. Santi exchanged a neat one-two with Nicky Butt and then struck a ferocious shot, which stayed low and went under the outstretched arms of the diving Petr Cech.

It was a sensational goal, one that was destined to win television's Goal of the Month competition, and it stunned the Stamford Bridge faithful into near silence.

When half time came soon after, the travelling Toon Army supporters were still buzzing with the quality of the Muñez strike.

But that was as good as it got for Newcastle. Chelsea came out in the second period and totally dominated, scoring through Lampard and Joe Cole. It could, and probably should, have been more, but the Newcastle youngsters defended heroically until the last minute.

Santi trudged wearily from the pitch. The following week was an 'international week', when players from the Premiership jetted off all over the globe to join their national squads for training and the first of several practice matches leading up to the World Cup tournament in the summer. Santi was relieved that his next match would be in the colours of Spain and grateful that the forthcoming weekend would give Newcastle some breathing space and a chance to get some of the injured players off the treatment tables and back onto the pitch.

Eight

'You look very nice,' said Roz, standing next to Santi and staring at his reflection in the full-length mirror.

'Nice?' said Santi, sounding concerned. 'I'm not sure that I should look *nice.*'

'Smart then,' said Roz quickly. 'Really smart, it's a lovely suit.'

'*Smart?*' said Santi, horrified. 'Smart is even worse than nice. There's no way I want to look *smart.*'

Roz rolled her eyes and sighed. 'Well, how exactly do you want to look then, Santi? Because I'm running out of words to describe how you look.'

Santi looked at himself in the mirror. 'I don't know. Er . . . maybe . . . er . . .'

'What?' said Roz, beginning to lose patience.

'Maybe . . . maybe . . . sort of . . . cool?'

Roz laughed. '*Cool!* Well, you do look cool, in a nice, smart sort of way.'

'But I told you, I don't want to look smart. It's not right.'

'Why did you put the suit on then?'

'Because you suggested it.'

'That was before I knew you didn't want to look smart. Look, Santi, you're going to a school to talk to the kids. If you'd feel better wearing jeans and a sweatshirt then do that.'

'But I don't want to look scruffy.'

Roz sighed again. 'I'm not suggesting you go the whole hog and turn up wearing a hoodie. Just wear what you feel comfortable and relaxed in.'

'But that's the problem. I don't feel comfortable, or relaxed. I'm really nervous, Roz, more nervous than if I were playing in a cup final.'

Roz smiled. She'd known all along that it wasn't really the clothes that were troubling her husband. But she couldn't resist teasing him a little about the event scheduled for later that day. 'But it's only ... what did the headteacher say ... only two hundred and fifty kids? You're used to playing in front of fifty thousand.'

'Yeah, but that's playing, not talking. And most of those fifty thousand are adults – not ... not ... *teenagers*.' The word emerged as though '*teenagers*' were the most dangerous species on the planet.

'They won't eat you, Santi,' said Roz, reading his mind and laughing to herself. 'You're just going to talk to them, and then they'll ask a few questions?'

'*Questions?* What sort of questions?'

'I don't know! How you started in the game, who your football heroes are? That sort of thing, I guess.'

Santiago's face went pale. 'I wish I'd never suggested it. I wanted to help Enrique, so I just said I'd do it, without really thinking. I didn't imagine it would actually happen.'

'You're joking, aren't you? They were bound to say yes. Famous footballer comes to talk to the kids. You'll have the local papers there and everything. Local telly too, most probably.'

'Oh, no,' said Santi miserably.

Roz put an arm around his shoulders and gave him a hug. 'You'll be great, the kids are gonna love you. And it's really good of you to do this for Enrique. It's obvious he's struggling with settling in at the school, even though he won't say anything. He'll appreciate you doing this.'

'Didn't seem like he appreciated it when he left this morning,' said Santi.

'Why, what did he say?'

'He just said, "Don't embarrass me," as he went out the door. As if I would.'

Roz laughed. 'He's nervous.' She kissed him on the cheek. 'Like his big brother. Now, you make yourself look *cool* and I'll go down and make us a quick lunch.'

'I don't think I can eat,' said Santi miserably. 'I've got stomachache and I feel sick. And I think I've got an asthma attack coming on.' He sighed as he looked at himself in the mirror and began to take off his suit jacket.

Roz smiled as she made her way down the stairs. 'Cool,' she said quietly.

The talk was going far better than Santi had expected, and after an uncertain few minutes at the beginning he had relaxed and was actually enjoying himself.

He was in the school hall, on the stage, with a microphone in his hand and two hundred and fifty school students staring up at him and hanging on his every word. It helped that almost every one of them, boys and girls, were Magpies fans to some degree or another.

The headteacher had made a big deal of the introduction and the fact that Santi was Enrique's brother. Enrique was at the end of a row, about halfway down the hall. He turned a vivid shade of crimson when the head asked him to stand up during his introduction and everyone in the hall turned and looked in his direction. Since then, like Santi, he had relaxed a little, as the talk was going well.

Santi had spoken about his love of football, the unusual way he had joined Newcastle United, his transfer to Real Madrid and his Champions League triumph. He'd even brought along his winners medal and had shown it to gasps of appreciation and a burst of applause.

Now the talk was reaching its conclusion. 'So, finally, I'd just like to say that I know I'm incredibly lucky to make my living playing a game I love, and I'll always be grateful to all the people who've helped me along the way. What I'm looking forward to now is playing in the World Cup and maybe' – he paused and smiled – 'maybe beating England in the final.'

There were a few good-natured jeers at that comment and Santiago laughed. 'Thanks very much for listening to me.'

The headteacher leaped to his feet and began to applaud vigorously. The kids joined in with the applause and added cheers and whistles of appreciation. After about a minute the head-teacher gestured for the clapping to stop and the room eventually went silent. 'Now,' he said, 'Mr Muñez is an extremely busy man, but he has kindly agreed to spend a few minutes answering some questions. So, who has the first one?'

A forest of hands shot up into the air. The head scanned the room and then pointed to a boy in the front row. 'Yes, Luke Thompson, ask your question.'

The first few questions were exactly the sort of thing Santiago expected and Roz had predicted: Who was Santi's favourite player? When, if ever, would Newcastle win the Premiership? The questions were simple to answer and the banter was friendly and amusing and Santi grew enough in confidence to pick out further questioners himself. He pointed to a boy sitting close to Enrique. 'What would you like to know?'

The boy was Jake Hodge, the leader of the gang that were doing their best to make Enrique's life a misery.

Jake grinned. 'How much do you earn a week?'

Maybe Santi should have expected a question like that, but he hadn't, and it wasn't something he wanted to go into. 'Er . . . er . . .'

Jake was ready with a follow up. 'Are you a multi-millionaire?'

Santi looked towards the headteacher, hoping that he would step in, but he had turned away for a moment – Santi had clearly been coping so well

– and was checking something with another member of staff.

'Enrique reckons you're a millionaire,' shouted Jake.

Santi pulled his thoughts together and came up with an answer. 'Like I said earlier, I'm very lucky to make my living playing a game I love. And it is a good living, yes.'

'Yeah, but is it right that you used to drive a Lamborghini?' shouted Jake's mate, Jordan Cole, joining in. 'What you got now, a Ferrari? Don't you think those sort of cars waste too much fuel? Our teachers keep telling us people should drive greener cars, not waste petrol on gas guzzlers. Is it one law for you lot and another for everyone else?'

Nearby, Enrique was sinking lower and lower into his chair. A lot of kids were laughing now, encouraging Jake and his mates to continue with the grilling.

'No, that's not right,' said Santi, much louder than he intended.

The headteacher turned at the sound and noticed immediately that the mood in the hall had changed drastically. He stood up. 'Right, that's all we have time for,' he said firmly. 'It just remains for us all to thank Mr Muñez once again for giving us all such an interesting and enlightening talk.'

Santiago breathed a sigh of relief and wiped the back of one hand across his forehead. He was sweating.

And out in the hall, Enrique was bitterly regretting ever having thought that this would be a good idea.

Nine

It was football, but not football like Gavin Harris had known or experienced for a good few years. He smiled and shook his head as he watched.

Gavin had grown accustomed to the ultimate in luxury during his time at Real Madrid – on the pitch, in the changing rooms, throughout the club and even at the training ground. The Bernabéu pitch was perfectly manicured and a delight to play on, the changing rooms were the ultimate in comfort with everything from gold-plated sinks to state-of-the-art treatment facilities; all around the stadium there was style and comfort. Even the training ground pitches were better than a lot of top-flight playing surfaces in the world.

But all that was behind Gavin now, for the time being at least. Being boss of a Spanish Segunda B side was another world, a million miles from the Champions League and champagne lifestyle at Real Madrid.

At Bardenas FC there was a new and compact little stadium, a generous and committed club owner, a small but enthusiastic group of players and a loyal fan base – all eight or nine thousand of them. But Gavin knew there could be many more if the club succeeded and continued to grow.

What Bardenas FC didn't have was multi-million Euro sponsorship, even more media money, a massive coaching and back-room staff, some of the world's top players, and a fan base that stretched from Madrid to every corner of the globe.

But Gavin didn't care. He was having the time of his life in northern Spain. It was back to basics – it had to be, because there was little money to spare. Gavin was manager and chief coach, but was happy to roll up his sleeves and help out with any little job around the club, ranging from answering the telephones to laying out the players' kits before a home match. On one occasion he'd even marked out the pitch when the groundsman took the day off to attend a niece's wedding. And Gavin was not only loving every minute of his new job, he was getting noticed as a potential major club manager of the future. Bardenas FC continued to challenge for a promotion play-off place and were still in the Copa del Rey – Spain's premier cup competition – making it all the way through to the round of sixteen and a chance to face one of the big guns from La Liga.

But Bardenas FC were facing an injury crisis of their own, and with a very small playing staff, Gavin was out and about in another of his roles – chief scout – looking for new and undiscovered talent.

He'd had a tip about a young and promising winger who was playing at a lower level but who was reckoned to be an undiscovered gem, missed or ignored by the scouts from the big clubs.

It was a Saturday afternoon and Gavin was standing on the touchline, one of a crowd of no more than three hundred. It was cold – Spain can get cold in the winter, especially northern Spain – and Gavin was wrapped in his overcoat. His Spanish girlfriend, Luisa, had accompanied him on the trip. She had one arm linked through Gavin's as they watched the match.

The standard of football being played ranged from below average to pretty awful; it was obvious why most of the guys out on the pitch were performing at this level. There was a lot of kick and rush, long balls, high balls, mis-kicked balls and downright bad balls, but there were very few good balls and very little finesse. There was only one exception, the guy Gavin had come to watch.

The tip had been spot on: the youngster had talent, raw talent for sure, but it was all there. And on top of that he had blistering pace, he was giving the full back and the entire opposition defence the total run around. The only thing missing was the final ball; his delivery was wayward to say the least, with maybe four out of five

crosses going anywhere but where they should –
into the box to threaten the back line and the
keeper. But that was something Gavin knew he
could work on and improve.

There was one other problem with the young
player; he was small, not very tall and quite
slight.

Gavin was deep in thought. He nodded as he
watched the winger nutmeg a defender and then
race on towards the goal. 'All right, he's small,
but being small hasn't stopped Aaron Lennon or
Shaun Wright-Phillips, has it?'

Gavin's girlfriend Luisa looked at him. 'Who?'

'Two English players, darling,' said Gavin
with a smile. 'They're small, like our friend out
there, but they're good – very good. And he
could be too.'

'You want to sign him then?' asked Luisa.

The winger sent in a cross and this time it was
perfect, only for the lumbering centre forward to
leap up and miss his header by a mile, not even
making contact with the ball.

Gavin smiled. 'You bet I want to sign him.'

Ten

'Well, what exactly is wrong with you?' asked Roz as she cleared away the breakfast dishes. As usual, she was in a hurry.

Enrique shrugged. 'I don't know, I just don't feel good.'

'Is it your head, your stomach? D'you feel nauseous?'

'What?'

'Sick? D'you feel sick?'

Enrique shrugged again. 'A bit, maybe. And . . . yeah, a headache. A bad headache.'

Little Rosie was sitting at the breakfast table, gazing at Enrique. 'Reekay's not well, Mummy.'

Roz closed the dishwasher and pressed the on button. 'Mmm, so he says, darling.'

'What d'you mean, "So he says"?' snapped Enrique.

'You were absolutely fine last night, playing with Rosie and—'

'So you don't want me to play with Rosie?' said Enrique, interrupting. 'Is that what you—?'

'I didn't say that, Enrique.'

The argument was getting heated and even Rosie was set on having her say. 'I want Reekay to play, Mummy.'

Roz sighed; it wasn't the greatest start to the day. 'I know, darling, and he will.'

This was exactly the sort of situation Roz had feared when Santi had suggested his half-brother come to live with them. With Santi away with the Spanish squad for over a week, she was left to run the house, do her job, look after their daughter *and* his teenage brother.

Roz thought to herself that it just wasn't fair, but at that moment she had no option but to get on with it, all of it. 'You'd better . . . go back to bed, I guess. Rest. See if you can sleep off whatever it is.'

'I'll be OK later,' said Enrique.

'We'll see. But you'll have to give the academy a miss this evening.'

'*No!* I can't miss the academy. We have a big game on the weekend.'

'Enrique, if you're not—'

'I'll be fine by tonight, I know I will.'

Roz didn't have time to continue the debate. She hurried out of the kitchen and returned a few moments later, wearing her coat and carrying Rosie's coat and shoes. 'My bag? Where did I leave my bag?'

Enrique stood up. 'Let me do Rosie's shoes while you find it.'

Roz nodded and handed over the shoes and the coat and went trudging off again. Enrique winked at little Rosie and swung her legs round from under the table so that he could start to put on and do up her shoes. The first one was in place when Roz returned clutching her bag.

'Found it.'

She watched Enrique as he went to secure the

second shoe, taking extra care not to pinch Rosie's foot as he pulled the strap tight, but not too tight.

'Enrique,' said Roz much more gently. 'Is everything . . . are you sure everything's OK at school?'

Enrique didn't reply for a moment. He couldn't tell Roz that school was far from OK. It was terrible, a nightmare. He couldn't tell her that far from making things better, Santi's visit to the school had ended up making things worse, much worse. He couldn't say that Jake Hodge and his mates had been targeting him even more as the rich brother of a big-shot footballer ever since the visit.

He couldn't say any of that. All he could say was, 'Sure it's OK. Why wouldn't it be OK? It's fine, it's very good.'

Rosie slid down from the chair, pulled on her coat, walked over to her mother and reached out to take her hand.

'Come on then, darling,' said Roz, opening the kitchen door. 'Time to go to Lorraine.' She looked at Enrique. 'I hope you feel better later.'

Enrique nodded and smiled weakly. 'Bye.'

Roz went out to the car, strapped Rosie into her seat and then got into the driver's seat. She secured her safety belt and started up the vehicle, thinking that she would speak to Santi about his brother that evening. Then she looked at Rosie in the rear-view mirror. She was waving to Enrique who was looking out of the window.

'There is something wrong,' said Roz as she pulled away. 'I know there is.'

Eleven

Fernando Torres drew his right foot back and unleashed a wicked shot with ferocious power. It flew like an arrow, straight and true, not deviating in the slightest in its flight, scorching past the outstretched arms of the diving José Reina and thumping into the net.

'Great shot, *El Nino*,' shouted someone from out on the pitch.

'He was lucky,' Reina bawled with a smile as he picked himself up and then picked up the ball from the back of the net. Torres, his Liverpool club-mate, looked back and grinned as he trotted back to the halfway line for the restart. The Spanish players were enjoying the practice match. It was hard work but fun as well, especially when one of them managed to get the better of a club-mate.

The manager and coaches were watching and taking notes, at times even joining in the light-hearted banter but always keeping in mind the serious work that lay ahead and the full-scale friendly international at the end of the week.

The ball was replaced on the spot and David Villa kicked off, prodding the ball to Santi who immediately passed it back to Andres Iniesta of Barcelona. Santi moved upfield, seeking out space to the left of and a little behind David Villa, concentrating on following the tactical instructions of the coaches.

With the World Cup finals looming ever closer, the international get-togethers and warm-up friendly matches were taking on an increasing importance and significance.

It was a vital time for both players and coaching staff. For the players, it was all about impressing their coaches with not only their skills but also their training, team spirit and overall attitude. Coaches, who spent most of the season watching their players from the directors' box of one league club or another, grabbed the opportunity of a few days working on and refining playing styles, formations and techniques.

The Spanish players had travelled to the international gathering from many different clubs in several different countries.

Every club manager has his own preferred playing style and formation, be it 4-4-2, 4-3-3, 4-2-3-1 or another of many possible permutations. On international duty, players had to adjust to a style that might be completely alien to them at their clubs. And they had to make that adjustment quickly and without fuss.

Santi had gradually established himself at international level, playing his part in World Cup qualifiers and in friendly matches. But most of his appearances had been as substitute; a place in the starting line-up was usually as a result of an injury to one of the established strikers. But Santi had one advantage over the other leading Spanish strikers – his favourite role was as second striker, playing a little deeper than out-and-out front men like Fernando Torres, David Villa and Dani Güiza.

It meant that should the manager go with a single striker and a five-man midfield, Santi was unlikely to get a starting role, but if the decision was to start with two up front, then Santi had a good chance of playing in the deeper role.

He was doing exactly that as the practice match continued, partnered with David Villa. The ball moved neatly through the midfield to Santi, who looked up and saw Villa's run. He threaded the ball through and Villa hit the shot on the run, bringing a fine save from Real Madrid's Iker Casillas, a former team-mate of Santi's.

Villa looked back to Santi, nodding and applauding the quality of the ball Santi had delivered.

This latest get-together was in Spain: a training week followed by a match against an opposition team similar in style to one of the teams in Spain's first round group at the World Cup finals. Spain would be facing Cameroon from the African qualifiers in their first group matches in South Africa, so the friendly against the Ivory Coast at the weekend would be a good test for the players.

Santi was hoping for a place in the starting line-up but if that didn't happen, he was desperate for a lengthy run-out from the bench. He'd been in fine form and the manager had watched him in the Premiership, seeing him score a couple of times.

Since winning the European Championships in 2008, the Spanish squad had bonded into a compact and close unit. Santi knew many of the squad very well, both from his time at Real Madrid, where a number of his former team-mates still played, and also from the English Premiership. Torres and Reina from Liverpool and Cesc Fàbregas from Arsenal were Premiership opponents, but for now club rivalries were forgotten, or at least put on hold, until after the international gathering was over.

The players were working intensively, with the coaches hammering home their tactics and trying various permutations from within the squad.

Little time was spent on fitness training; at this time of the season the players were already at peak fitness. It was all about getting the team working as a unit, not just the players who were virtually assured a starting place once the finals came around, but every member of the squad. They all needed to be ready. Anything could happen – injuries, loss of form, late arrivals to the squad. Every man in the squad wanted to play in the finals, not just to be there, so there was no chance of coasting through an international gathering. Maximum effort and concentration was not just required, it was demanded.

Out on the pitch, Santi was on a run, and this time David Villa was poacher turned provider, setting up Santi with a deft touch through the defence. Santi had anticipated the pass well; the understanding was growing through all areas of the Spanish squad. He took the ball on for a couple of strides and then thumped it past Casillas. It wasn't as stunning a strike as the one Torres had scored a few minutes before, but it was a well-worked and well-taken goal.

Santi smiled as he looked over to the touchline and saw the coaches nodding their satisfaction and then making notes. Good. If he was giving them selection headaches he was delighted.

Twelve

Enrique couldn't get used to this English weather; it felt as though winter would never end. It was bitterly cold, again, and the freezing air snatched at Enrique's lungs and mingled with his icy breath.

But despite the cold and the freezing air, Enrique still felt good. He always did when he was on a football pitch. His worries and problems faded away when he had a football at his feet and was playing the beautiful game.

The under-16 squad at the academy played regular matches against other clubs for the north of England in the Premier Academy League. At this stage in the young footballers' careers all the games were friendly matches – there was no league table or no end of season play-offs. League tables would come if and when the youngsters stepped up to under-18 level. But none of that stopped the under-16 squad from working out exactly where they would be placed if there *had* been an official league table.

And the Newcastle youngsters knew they would be up there challenging for top spot. They were having a good season and Enrique was only making them better. Every match, even training matches, mattered to him. There was really no such thing as a friendly; he hated to lose, he even hated to draw.

The team were playing against Liverpool academy, and as always it was a fiercely competitive match. There was no score but Enrique was really getting stuck in, as well as urging on his team-mates with shouts of encouragement and handclaps.

Enrique was covering more of the pitch than anyone: engineering attacks, steadying the mid-field, helping out in defence. When the Newcastle keeper failed to catch a goal-bound shot cleanly Enrique was there to hook it away to safety. Once he saw the danger was over he turned back and gave the keeper a mouthful, telling him that *he* could have dealt with the ball easily and that if the keeper couldn't manage in goal *he* would step in and do the job properly. Fortunately, he said it all in Spanish and the keeper had no idea what he was on about.

Enrique's team-mates were getting used to his outbursts in his own language, and most of the time they just laughed at them. That was mainly because they all admired their Spanish team-mate as a player, for his stamina, his skill, and most of all for his determination. The academy players were used to being around the club's superstars so there was no question of anyone being over-awed by the fact that he was the half-brother of Santiago Muñez. They just liked and respected Enrique because he was good and because he had slipped seamlessly into being one of the squad, part of it all.

And Enrique knew it, and he wished it could be the same at school. He wished he could go back to day one and start the whole thing over again. But he couldn't.

As he jogged back towards the halfway lines, his thoughts suddenly drifted to school. The previous day had been horrible, from the moment he'd arrived. Missing a day hadn't helped; if anything Jake and the others had picked on him even more than usual to make up for lost time. By lunch time, Enrique had had enough. He'd slipped out of the main gates and spent the rest of the afternoon wandering around town. But it couldn't continue that way. He knew it couldn't.

'Enrique!'

He didn't hear the shout. He didn't see the high ball drop down and bounce on the hard ground just in front of him and then sail over his head and fall obligingly into the path of one of the Liverpool attackers.

'*Enrique!*'

He came out of the dream and for a fleeting moment thought he was somewhere else, at school. Then his brain cleared and he knew exactly where he was.

'Pick him up, Enrique! He's in.'

Enrique turned and saw the striker racing away towards goal. He gave chase but knew already that he was too late. He'd been caught napping, and his defence had been caught out of position, thinking that Enrique had the space covered.

The striker exchanged a neat one-two with one of his team-mates and thumped in a well-placed shot that beat the keeper low down in one corner.

Enrique checked his run and gazed up to the sky in frustration just as the keeper picked the ball out of the net. He turned and glared at Enrique. Words were not necessary; Enrique knew exactly what the keeper was thinking.

He looked over to the touchline. The academy coach wasn't looking too happy either.

Thirteen

'Do you want to speak to Rosie?'

'Of course I do.'

Roz smiled and held the telephone to her daughter's ear and for the next minute listened to a mainly one-sided conversation from Santiago.

It was a day off for Roz and she was delighted to be at home with Rosie. Santi had arranged to phone while Rosie was still up so that he could speak to her.

When Rosie had run out of things to say to her dad, she muttered, 'Bye, bye', gave the phone to Roz, slipped off her lap and tottered off to find some of her toys.

Roz put the phone to her ear. 'She didn't have a lot to say to you.'

'It's just good to hear her voice,' said Santiago at the other end of the call.

'How's it all going?'

'Great. The training's been really good, and I'll definitely play part of the match tomorrow. Not sure how much yet, we don't know the starting line-up.'

Roz paused before she replied. 'Right.'

'Roz, is there something wrong?'

'Er . . . not really. I'm OK. Why do you ask?'

'Look, I know you're not the greatest football fan in the world, but you could show a little interest. You seem so distant, a million miles away.'

'Santi, I'm sorry. I'm really sorry.'

'So what is it?'

Roz sighed. She hadn't meant to start this conversation; she didn't want to worry Santi just before a hugely important match. But there was no choice now. 'It's . . . it's Enrique.'

She could hear the anxiety in Santi's voice as he spoke. 'Has something happened? Has he been hurt?'

'No,' said Roz quickly. 'No, he's fine. Physically, at least.'

'Roz, I don't know what you're talking about. What's going on?'

Roz quickly told Santi about Enrique's sudden 'illness' which had miraculously cleared up by the time he was due to go to the academy.

'And it's been getting worse since then. He just doesn't want to go to school. I'm sure there's something going on.'

'What? What could be going on? Is it a teacher? Is he having problems with his lessons?'

'I . . . I don't think so. I think it's something else. He won't say anything, but I think—'

'What? What is it you think?'

'I think he might be being bullied.'

Santi said nothing for a few moments and Roz knew he was weighing up what she had said.

'Do you think I should speak to him tonight?' he said finally. 'Shall I call back later when he's home?'

'No,' said Roz. 'I don't want you to worry about this. Not now, not just before such an important game.'

'But I *am* worried.'

'Yes, I know but try not to be. I didn't mean for us to talk about it now, it just slipped out.

'I will call later.'

'No,' said Roz emphatically. 'No, you need to relax tonight, and rest. It'll wait 'til you get home.'

'If you're sure . . .'

'I *am*. Honestly. Maybe I'm worrying too much anyway. Maybe it's nothing at all.'

'Well . . . OK then. Listen, Roz, I have to go, we all eat together on these trips and no one is allowed to duck out.'

Roz laughed. 'All right, you go and have dinner with the boys.'

'I love you, Roz. Give Rosie a kiss from me.'

'I love you too. And I will.'

'Bye, Roz.'

'Santi . . . ?'

'What?'

'Good luck with the match tomorrow.'

Fourteen

The Ivory Coast players were giving the Spanish a thorough workout. They were a big, physical team, not afraid to put it about, and just the type of team that could make things difficult for the generally smaller and more nimble Spanish.

With a playing style that was fast and direct, very similar to the Cameroon side Spain would be facing at the World Cup, this was an excellent test. And it was tough, very tough, particularly as the Ivory Coast had Premiership players Kolo Touré, Emmanuel Eboué and Didier Drogba in its line-up.

Santi, to his surprise but to his great delight, had been on from the kick-off, partnering

Fernando Torres up front. And the partnership was operating as smoothly as the one Santi had forged with David Villa during the training match.

The movement was clever and incisive, both strikers seeming to instinctively know when and where his partner would time and make a run. The problem was that chances were very thin on the ground and when the front men did get a sniff of goal, the big Ivory Coast defenders were not slow to arrive with a heavy tackle.

Santi had seen a rasping shot tipped over the bar by the keeper and Torres had sent a bullet header fractionally wide on an upright.

But they were the only clear chances that had fallen to the two front men. And the Ivory Coast had almost taken the lead themselves on a couple of occasions. Casillas had made a great stop from close range and Spain's own big man, Sergio Ramos, had intercepted a goal-bound header just in time.

It was a fast and fascinating match and Santi was enjoying every moment of it – much more, it appeared, than sections of the Spanish crowd were.

Now that Spain were reigning European champions, the expectations and the demands of their fervent supporters had risen. Across the world, Spain were reckoned to be one of the favourites for the World Cup; across Spain, they were a nailed-on certainty.

So with more than thirty of the first forty-five minutes gone and the match still goalless, certain sections of the crowd were becoming restless.

There were a few whistles of derision as a Spanish attack broke down and high up in the stands, behind one goal, a small group started a slow handclap, which fortunately wasn't picked up by the rest of the crowd.

The bulk of the Spanish supporters were fiercely loyal to their team, and were prepared to be patient. But not for ever. They wanted a goal, and they wanted it now.

Santiago Muñez was about to provide it.

Cesc Fàbregas had the ball out wide. He looked up and saw the runs of his strikers, Torres and Muñez. Fàbregas slipped the ball infield to Xavi, who played it first time to Torres. The striker held off a muscular challenge and, slightly off balance, managed to play the ball back towards Santi.

Santi was moving at pace – all reason said that he should never really have got a proper touch on the ball, let alone do what he did with it. It was going behind him, no doubt. Somehow though, he managed to dig it out with his right foot and send a ferocious shot across the face of the goal, past the stunned keeper, who didn't even have time to dive, and into the net.

The crowd roared as one, all signs of protest drowned out in rapturous cheers and applause as Santi ran across the turf, one arm raised, Alan Shearer like, with his team-mates chasing after him.

It was a great goal and up in one of the stands Gavin Harris, taking time out from his club duties, was on his feet, cheering and applauding like every other Spanish fan around him.

'That's my boy, Santi,' Gavin shouted. 'That's my boy!'

Everyone in the Spanish dressing room knew there would be changes at half time. That's what these warm-up matches were all about, giving most of the squad the chance to get on and show what they could do.

So when the Spanish went out to start the second half Santi was expecting that he would be taking up residence on the bench while another striker took the field to do his stuff. But he wasn't.

The management team knew exactly what Torres and Villa could do in tandem; they'd seen them operate together many times. Santi was the relative newcomer – they needed to take a good look at him in match conditions, seeing him working with at least one more of their established front men.

So when the second half began, Santi was still there, this time alongside David Villa. Santi realized exactly why he'd been kept on and he didn't expect to play the whole half. Dani Güiza was almost certain to get a runout at some time, but Santi was determined to make the most of it, and enjoy however many more minutes he was going to have on the pitch.

The half started well, with Villa and Muñez

picking up where they'd left off in training, and operating as successfully as Torres and Muñez had in the first half. The Spanish as a whole were playing with more confidence, having got used to the physicality of the Ivory Coast team.

But the Ivory Coast weren't just there to make up the numbers; they also had moves and tactics to perfect and players to try out.

A couple of new young defenders came on, with fresh legs and the determination to prove that they should have been there from the start.

After that the match became tight again, the spaces closed down and there were few, if any, real scoring opportunities for either team.

Santi was getting no joy from his new marker, who had little finesse but bucketloads of brute strength and controlled aggression. He wasn't a dirty player, just clumsy and awkward, and Santi had twice found himself flat out on the deck in the few brief but memorable minutes the newcomer had been on the pitch.

Santi glanced over at the touchline, saw that Dani Güiza was warming up and knew that his match was almost over. That was fine, it had all gone better than he could ever have imagined. But as he saw the ball spin free from a midfield tussle, he thought that maybe, just maybe, there might be a chance to leave an even greater impression on the match.

He darted towards the ball, and the defender, wrong-footed for a moment, regained his balance and went lumbering after him like a charging rhinoceros.

Santi moved out towards the wing, intending to cut in late and test the keeper with a long-range curling effort. He could already see the shot in his mind; he just had to create the position to take it.

The defender, awkward but swift, chased in pursuit with a long gangling stride that ate up the yards.

Santi found the space to cut inside, switching direction skilfully and effortlessly. The defender didn't have the same skill and as Santi drew back his right foot to hit the shot, his opponent came racing in at full steam and was unable to stop his own right foot from landing on Santi's left.

It was a complete and total accident, very

similar to the one that happened to Wayne Rooney back in 2004 at the European Championships in the match against Portugal.

And as Santi's agonized scream echoed around the stadium, everyone there – players, supporters, coaches, press and television commentators and pundits, and Santi's best mate Gavin Harris – were desperately hoping that this incident would not have the same terrible outcome.

Fifteen

'I'm sorry, I'm afraid it isn't good news; there is a break in the fourth metatarsal.'

Santiago slumped back on the hospital bed, put both hands to his head and groaned. It was all so horribly familiar – a terrible injury as the World Cup finals were approaching. Last time, back in 2006, an injury had prevented him from playing any part in the finals, and now, with a metatarsal break – an injury that all footballers dread – it looked as though lightning really was going to strike in the same place twice.

Santi's thoughts flew back to the summer of 2006 and the last World Cup finals. He'd been at home, with Roz, watching the matches on TV, nursing a broken arm sustained in a stupid training ground accident. The heavy plaster cast had been with him throughout the most frustrating few weeks of his entire life, seeing his friends, club-mates and opponents, all playing in the greatest tournament in football while he could do nothing more than watch.

And now it looked as though it could be happening all over again. There were still four months to the finals but metatarsal breaks could take many months to heal completely.

Wayne Rooney had suffered the injury twice – firstly to the fifth metatarsal and then to the fourth – and many other top players had also suffered metatarsal breaks. David Beckham, Steven Gerrard, Ledley King, Gary Neville and Michael Owen were just a few of the famous players who had struggled for months to recover. And now the name of Santiago Muñez could be added to that illustrious list.

Santiago was hardly listening; his thoughts were all about his World Cup dreams being shattered as the specialist continued to speak.

'The bone will take some time to recover, but in some ways you have been fortunate.'

'What?' said Santi, hearing the word, 'fortunate'. 'How do you work that out? How could I have been *fortunate?*'

The specialist spoke slowly; he wanted to ensure that Santi knew exactly what lay ahead. 'Metatarsals are the five long bones in the fore-foot; they connect the ankle bones to the bones in the toes. The first metatarsal is linked to the big toe and the fifth links to the little toe. With me so far?'

Santi nodded. 'Yeah.'

'And the metatarsals act as a unit, to help share the load of the body. They move position to cope with uneven ground.'

'You said I'd been fortunate,' said Santi impatiently. 'What exactly does that mean?'

The specialist wasn't going to be rushed. 'The fourth is one of the inner bones,' answered the specialist calmly.

'I worked that one out for myself.'

'Which means,' continued the specialist com-pletely unruffled, 'that its recovery can be aided by a sort of splint effect of the bones on either side.'

Santi said nothing for a moment, slowly taking in the information he had been given. 'So . . . the break could clear up more quickly than if it was an outer metatarsal?'

The specialist nodded. 'Exactly. It *could*, but it will be a long process.'

'How long?'

'I can't predict that. Not yet,' said the specialist.

'But . . . but the World Cup finals, they start in fifteen or sixteen weeks. Do I have a chance of playing?'

The specialist didn't answer.

'I've got to know,' said Santi urgently. 'Do I have a chance?'

'I'm making no promises,' said the specialist eventually, 'but, yes, you have a chance.'

Sixteen

Enrique's school had an anti-bullying policy, which was taken very seriously by all the staff and almost all the pupils. It involved older kids monitoring the younger ones, watching and listening for any signs or signals of bullying.

But the system could only work if the person being bullied gave those signs or made those signals. Enrique was determined to do neither – his pride wouldn't let him admit to anyone that he was being bullied again and he was making certain that none of the other kids at school suspected what was happening.

Part of the problem was that he hadn't made a particular friend or group of friends at the school. He was so wrapped up in his football that making friends had taken a back seat while he tried to establish himself at the academy. So at school, Enrique was regarded as a bit of a loner. And Jake Hodge, Jordan Cole and Craig Cameron were making the most of that situation.

It was lunch time and Enrique had slipped away from school to buy himself a sandwich at a small corner shop. There was nothing wrong with that, pupils were allowed out at lunch times if they didn't want a school lunch. And the shop was in a quiet part of town, a fair walk away from school, and from his three tormentors.

But Enrique was feeling a little better than he had for a while. Jake and his friends had mostly ignored him during the morning. Even during the morning break, when they'd spotted him alone, they'd just walked on by without even bothering to throw in a couple of insults.

As he walked from the shop carrying a sandwich in a paper bag, Enrique was wondering if maybe they'd grown tired of taunting and tormenting him

But they hadn't.

As Enrique delved into the bag to take out his sandwich he heard footsteps running towards him from behind. Before he could turn around he felt the bag snatched from his hand.

It was Jake Hodge, and he wasn't alone. Jordan Cole and Craig Cameron were with him.

Jake turned back and laughed as he reached into the bag and took out half of the sandwich. 'Look, lads, tuna and cucumber on wholemeal bread. That's very healthy and nutritious.' He stared at Enrique. 'Is this what makes you big and strong, Enrique?'

Enrique said nothing.

'He's not looking too strong to me,' laughed Jordan. 'More like a bit of a wimp.'

'Aye,' said Craig, joining in the banter. 'Maybe we should try some of that tuna. Give us a bite, Jake lad.'

Enrique watched as Jake ripped one half of the sandwich down the middle and handed one piece to Jordan and the other to Craig. They both bit into the bread and chewed very deliberately as they stared at Enrique.

'Delicious,' said Jordan through a mouthful of tuna.

'Oh, aye,' laughed Craig. 'That's special. I'll ask the old lady to get some in.'

Jake took the other half of sandwich from the bag and took a single, small bite. 'No, I don't like it. Actually, I think it's disgusting.' He dropped the remaining part of the sandwich onto the pavement but then grinned at Enrique. 'Oh, sorry, did you want some of that?' Still smiling, he bent down and picked up the sandwich. Jake moved closer to Enrique, holding the sandwich at arm's length. 'You love this stuff, don't you? Here, take a bite.'

Enrique edged backward, shaking his head. The only way they'd get him to eat the sandwich now was by forcing him. The trouble was that all three boys had stopped smiling and laughing; it looked as though they might very well do exactly that.

'You three, you make me sick,' said Enrique bravely. 'Not one of you would do this if you were on your own.'

'That's 'cos there's safety in numbers, see,' said

Jordan, grinning. 'That's an old English saying.'

Quickly Enrique reached into a jacket pocket and pulled out a can of drink he'd also bought in the shop. He drew back his arm and glared at Jake, silently challenging him to come closer.

Jake just grinned and pulled the sandwich away from Enrique's face. 'There's another old English saying you should know; if you can't beat 'em, join 'em.'

'I don't know what you mean,' said Enrique, lowering his arm a little.

Jake threw the bread and tuna down into the gutter. 'Come with us. We'll show you what it means.'

Seventeen

Santiago looked away from the window. Little more than a week had passed since his injury and he was already sick of spending endless hours staring out at the same trees, the same piece of lawn, the same long drive leading down to the same gates. His home had become like a prison, especially when he was on his own.

'Rest it. Complete rest.' That was the main order he'd been given. 'Keep off the foot. No exercise at all for at least four, and maybe eight weeks.' He'd heard that from specialists, the national team doctor, the club doctor, the physio, and even from Roz, whose medical training meant she knew a fair amount about metatarsal breaks.

Santi was wearing a removable plastic cast so that the break was immobilized. This meant the cast could be removed for physiotherapy treatment, which would prevent stiffness in his foot and ankle. Santi was doing exactly as he'd been ordered, following his instructions to the letter. And it was driving him crazy. That meant he was being a pain to Roz, and Enrique, and even to little Rosie. But all he could think about was that it looked as though he would miss his second World Cup in succession through injury, and that maybe his last chance of ever playing in the finals was gone.

And the injury was having repercussions in many areas. The club management were not happy that he had picked up the injury while on international duty. It was a risk all clubs with international players in their ranks were faced with. But footballers wanted to represent their countries and they couldn't be wrapped in cotton wool, no matter what their club managers felt.

The St James' Park faithful were even more incensed. With the ongoing injury crisis, Santi had been the mainstay of the fans' hopes for the season; his performances could have made the difference between the Magpies finishing the season in a respectable Premiership position or down in the bottom half of the table. Now he was out, almost certainly for the remainder of the season, when the team could least afford to lose him.

Internet chat sites and message boards were full of furious comment and words of protest from angry supporters. Santi didn't usually bother much with checking out the sites, but to ease the boredom of not training or playing he had looked at a few, and they didn't make good reading.

This was the second time Santi had suffered a broken bone in the leg. That, added to his broken arm and the succession of injuries he had suffered at Real Madrid had caused one supporter to dub him 'Sicknote Muñez'. It was a nickname once given to the former Spurs and England winger Darren Anderton, who was plagued by injuries for much of his career. And it was a nickname Santi didn't want.

He was thinking about it as he slumped back

on the sofa. He sighed; he wasn't good at spending so much time alone.

The familiar sound of Roz's car broke into his gloomy thoughts. He sat up. 'OK, Muñez,' he said quietly, 'be calm, be nice.'

He hadn't been either calm or particularly nice over the past few days. He was angry, with himself as much as anything, and he'd been taking it out on everyone around him, especially those closest to him and Roz was closest of all. He had to try to be more reasonable and less short-tempered.

He smiled as Roz came into the room, holding Rosie by the hand. 'Hello, princess,' he said to Rosie, who gave him one of her sunniest smiles. Santi turned to Roz. 'And how's my other princess?'

'Long day,' Roz replied. 'And busy.' She came over and kissed Santi. 'How about you?'

'Driver picked me up, took me for treatment, then back here. Every day's the same right now. Oh, and Gavin called about an hour ago. To see how I was doing and to tell me how well his team are playing.'

'I'm glad he called.'

'He's a good friend.'

'You've got a lot of good friends.'

'I haven't seen much of them.'

Roz and Santi were both being cautious about what they said. It wasn't natural to them, but Roz felt that being around Santi had been like walking on eggshells for the past week. She had to tread delicately. 'To be fair, Santi,' she said now, 'that's mainly down to you. You've not exactly been welcoming to visitors, you hardly said a word when Jamie came round.'

'It's hard for me to talk to Jamie.'

'Hard? He and Gavin are your best friends.'

'Yeah, but . . .'

'What?'

Santi sighed. 'My injury is bad, really bad, I know that. But I'll get over it, even if I do miss the World Cup.' He paused for a moment. 'But Jamie . . .'

'I know,' Roz said, sitting next to him and taking his hands in hers. They both watched Rosie happily playing on the carpet with one of her toys for a few moments. 'But Jamie's football career ended before it had really begun,' she added softly.

Santi nodded. 'I've got no right to moan and feel sorry for myself when I'm with Jamie.'

'Even when,' said Roz with a smile, 'what you really want to do *is* moan and feel sorry for yourself.'

Santi nodded again. 'You noticed?'

'Just a bit.'

'I'm sorry, Roz.'

'I know you are. And you know that you've got no option but to be patient. Everyone will do everything they can to get you to the World Cup. And I'm here to support you, and so are friends like Jamie.'

'Yeah, you're right.'

'Why don't you give him a call? Ask him to come over tonight. I know he won't mind if you have a *little* moan. But not for too long.'

'Yeah. Yeah, I will. Thanks, babe.'

'All part of the service,' said Roz with a smile. She kissed him on the cheek and pushed herself up from the sofa. 'And now I am going to have a long, hot soak in the bath while you keep an eye on our darling daughter.'

'My pleasure.'

Roz walked towards the door but then stopped and turned back. 'Oh, by the way, where's Enrique?'

'I don't know. He's not come back from school yet.'

Roz thought for a few moments. 'Mmm. He's been late back a lot recently. Seems a bit happier though, I think.' She shrugged her shoulders. 'Even after nearly four months with us, I'm still never quite sure with Enrique.'

Eighteen

Enrique slipped the DVD into the inside pocket of his jacket, certain that no one had seen him do it. He didn't move on but stayed at the rack, apparently looking through the selection, taking his time like any normal shopper.

The shop was busy, and after a couple of minutes Enrique moved on. But instead of going straight for the exit he paused at another rack and looked again, like he had just spotted something he wanted. He lifted out a DVD, examined it for a few moments and then slid it back into position.

This time, when he moved, he walked casually out through the exit door. It was a small, independent shop, not one of the big chain stores. There were no CCTV cameras and no security tabs on the products to set off the alarm at the doorway, so as Enrique made his way down the street he knew he'd got away with it.

Jake and Jordan were waiting on the corner.

'Did you get it?' asked Jake.

Enrique nodded.

'Let's have a look then?'

'Not here,' said Enrique quickly. 'We don't know who's watching.'

Just then Craig, the third member of the gang, came strolling up. He nodded to Jake.

Jake grinned. 'You're good,' he said to Enrique. 'And I reckon you've done this before.'

Enrique was burning inside with shame. But Jake was right, he had stolen before. Many times, too many times.

In Madrid, Enrique's parents Rosa-Maria and Miguel ran a small bar in one of the poorer parts of the city. It was a tough neighbourhood – just making a living and getting by was difficult. Back then Enrique didn't even know he had a famous half-brother. Life was hard. His parents were busy, and they didn't notice at first when their son started stealing.

It wasn't only down to Enrique – an older kid was bullying him and ordering him to steal. Enrique got away with the stealing for quite a while, but in the end he was found out.

Now it was happening all over again, and rather than finding a way out by standing up to the bullies, Enrique had decided to take the easy option by stealing again. That way he could win the bullies' friendship, but at the same time he knew he would lose every last atom of self-respect.

He handed over the DVD to Jake, knowing he was risking everything and that this time there was so much more to lose. If the truth came out he'd be suspended from school and thrown out of the academy. His dreams would be shattered for ever; he would never get to be a professional foot-baller and his parents and half-brother would feel betrayed and would never forgive him.

As he watched Jake pocket the DVD, the full stupidity of what he had just done hit him with the strength of a sledgehammer.

Jake grinned. 'We'll find something a lot more interesting for you to do tomorrow.' He started to move off. 'Come on.'

Jordan and Craig went to follow but Enrique stood his ground. 'I said, come on,' said Jake. 'Let's go.'

Enrique shook his head. 'I'm going nowhere, not with you three. What I did just then was stupid; I don't know why I did it. Yes, yes, I do. It was so you'd stop pushing me around, so you'd be my friends. But I don't want friends like you. I must be crazy. I'd sooner have no friends than you three.'

'Is that right?' said Jake. He looked at his two friends. 'And we were getting on so well, weren't we lads?'

'Aye,' nodded Jordan.

'We were that,' agreed Craig. 'Best mates, I'd say.'

'I was crazy,' said Enrique angrily. 'I'll never steal again, not for you or anyone. And you can do what you want to me, I don't care.'

'Oh, you'll do exactly as we tell you, Enrique,' said the grinning Jake. 'You wouldn't want the school, or the academy, or even big brother to find out what you've just done, would you?'

Enrique glared at the grinning Jake. 'You say what you want and I'll say you're lying. They'll believe me before they believe you three.'

'We don't have to *say* anything, do we, lads?' Jake said to the others.

'Oh, no, we don't have to *say* a word,' said Jordan. 'We'll just show 'em the evidence.'

'Evidence?' said Enrique. 'You mean the DVD? Anyone could have taken that. Any one of you could have stolen it.'

Jake laughed. 'Show him, Craig.'

Craig reached into a pocket and took out his cellphone. He pressed a couple of buttons and then held out the phone so that Enrique could see the video that was running.

There he was in the shop, in perfect focus, slipping the DVD into his pocket.

Enrique felt himself go cold and the hairs on the back of his neck stood up. Craig had captured the whole thing on his phone's video.

Jake was laughing. 'See you tomorrow, pal,' he said to Enrique. 'Same time same place.'

Nineteen

The bone had knitted together, the two broken pieces fusing in the mysterious, almost magical way that broken bones mend.

According to the doctors the recovery was progressing exactly as expected, Santi just had to be patient. That was a problem; patience had never been one of Santi's strongest qualities.

He'd just about managed to stay patient during the four long weeks he'd worn the plastic boot, stopping himself time and time again from testing out the strength of his foot by placing it on the ground and applying a little pressure.

He'd somehow remained patient during end-less sessions of hydrotherapy in the swimming pool, sessions when he didn't even swim but just did exercises, non weight-bearing exercises.

He'd kept patient when freezing ice packs were wrapped around his foot and when mini oxygen tents were used.

It had been like a trip to hell but somehow, in some way, Santi had stayed patient.

But now at last, finally, the boot was off, training could start and Santi's supply of patience was just about exhausted. He wanted to run, jump, kick a ball, leap high in the air, throw himself into a tackle, even though – like most strikers – tackling was just about the weakest aspect of his game.

He wanted to do all those things. But he wasn't doing any of them. He was in the club gym, sitting on an exercise bicycle, pedalling, clocking up the miles and applying just the amount of pressure the coaches and doctors said he could. But it *was* training, at last, strengthening his foot and leg muscles and giving him his first aerobic workout in what seemed like an age.

One of the club's coaches, a former player by the name of Les, had been appointed to watch over Santi and monitor his progress. He was fussing around like a mother hen with her favourite chick as Santi increased the speed and applied a little more pressure on the pedals. 'Take it easy, Santi, you're not in the Tour de France.'

Santi laughed. 'Bring it on. I never knew being on a bike could feel so good.'

'Yeah, well, this just gets your body working again. We'll gradually build up the muscle strength and your lung capacity.'

It wasn't much, just a ride on an exercise bike, but it felt fantastic. Through the windows of the exercise room, Santi could see other members of the first-team squad and the reserves being put through their paces out on the practice pitches. He turned back to Les and gestured towards the players outside. 'How long before I'm out there with them?'

Les shrugged. 'Let's not run before you can walk, eh.'

'But I can walk. And I can ride a bike without falling off. Come on, how long?'

Les knew that there was still a long way to go, and that there would be plenty of downs as well as ups before Santi regained full fitness. 'I don't know, Santi, let's see how it is in a couple of weeks.'

'A couple of weeks! But—'

'You just gotta be . . .'

'Yeah, I know,' said Santi with a laugh.

They said it together, 'Patient!'

Training had never felt so good, even though he had done nothing more than a gentle warm-up followed by the ride on a bike going nowhere.

But when it was over, as Santi took a shower, he was feeling better and more optimistic than he had in a long time. There was still time to make the World Cup finals. He'd do everything he could to get there and he knew the Spanish manager and his team were going to give him every chance to make it. They had been in regular touch, checking on his progress and offering words of encouragement.

There were numerous examples of players who'd come back from a metatarsal break amazingly quickly; some, like Wayne Rooney and David Beckham, possibly too quickly.

Others had made almost miraculous recoveries. David Nugent had been playing for Preston North End when he broke his fifth metatarsal, one of the worst of the bones to break. But six weeks later he had been back in first-team action, saying that his remedy was to drink plenty of milk.

Santi had read all he could about metatarsal breaks and he'd drunk plenty of milk. And he'd also spoken with lots of other pros who had suffered the same injury and was amazed and touched at the support, advice and encouragement he was given.

He was feeling great as he walked from the training ground. His phone rang and he glanced at the screen and saw that the call was from Gavin. He flipped open the phone. 'Hey, man, how you doing?'

'I'm good.' Gavin had obviously noticed Santi's cheery greeting. 'And you're sounding pretty good too.'

'I feel it. I feel great. I started training again today. Only in the gym, but it's still training.'

'Hey, Santi, that's brilliant, man. You'll make the World Cup, I know you will.'

Santi laughed. 'I'm gonna do my best.'

'You'd better. I told you before, I want you there with me. And I've got some news of my own, good news.'

'Don't tell me you and Luisa are getting married?'

This time Gavin laughed. 'Don't rush me. No, not yet, but maybe in the future . . .'

'So what is it then,' said Santi, 'this news of yours?'

'You know we're the only lower leagues team still in the of the Copa del Rey?'

'Of course I know, you've told me every time you've won a match.'

'Yeah, well the draw for the quarterfinals was made today. And who do you think we got?'

Santi thought for a moment. 'Not . . . ? Surely you didn't get . . . ?'

Gavin laughed loudly. 'Oh, yes we did. We drew Real Madrid. Gavin Harris is going back to the Bernabéu!'

Twenty

Breakfast time in the Muñez household could be a hectic time, especially if Roz was on the early shift at the hospital and had to drop off Rosie at Lorraine's on the way to work.

Roz was hurrying around, getting ready to go, while Santi and Enrique sat at the table. Santi was drinking a coffee and reading the sports pages of the morning paper and Enrique was pushing cereal around a bowl rather than actually eating any of it.

Enrique looked deep in thought and Roz noticed it as she picked up Rosie to leave. 'You all right, Enrique?'

He didn't answer.

'Reekay!'

This time Enrique heard. He looked up and saw Rosie smiling at him, arms outstretched, waiting for a kiss goodbye. He stood up and kissed Rosie on the cheek. 'Have a good time. See you later.' He smiled at Roz, who was looking concerned.

'Are you all right?' she asked again.

Enrique nodded. 'Sure. Fine.'

Roz didn't look completely convinced, but she didn't have time to discuss it. She carried Rosie around the table to Santi, who was totally engrossed in reading reports of the previous night's FA Cup replays.

'Bye, Santi.'

Santi looked up. 'Oh, sorry, darling, I was reading the Liverpool report. Torres scored again for Liverpool.'

'Good for Torres,' said Roz. 'But we have to leave.'

'Course you do. I'll walk you out to the car.'

Santi took his daughter from Roz and they walked out to Roz's car together. Santi strapped

Rosie into her seat, kissed her goodbye and closed the door firmly.

'Drive safely,' he said to Roz.

'Course,' Roz replied. 'Listen, Santi, have a word with Enrique before you go. He's been looking worried again lately.'

'Has he?'

Roz sighed. 'I know you're concentrating on playing again, but I think your brother needs some attention too.'

'OK. I'll talk to him. I'm sorry I've been a bit obsessive about—'

Roz leaned forward and stopped Santi with a kiss. 'I know,' she said. 'And I understand, but have a word with him. Now, I have to go.'

She got into the car and Santi watched her drive away, waving at Rosie, who kept waving back until the car had disappeared from view.

Then he went inside. Enrique was at the dishwasher, stacking the breakfast dishes. He pushed the door shut and turned to see Santiago staring at him.

'What's wrong?' Enrique asked.

'Nothing with me. How about you?'

Enrique could barely look his brother in the eyes. He hesitated for a moment. 'Is this Roz? Did she ask you to say this to me?'

'She worries. About me, and Rosie, and about you. You're one of the family.'

Hearing that made everything even worse for Enrique. The past few weeks had been a night-mare, with Jake and his friends dragging Enrique deeper and deeper into their world and their ways.

He'd stolen again for them several times more – nothing huge, but that didn't matter. It was the principle of what he was doing. It was wrong and he was deeply ashamed of himself. But he couldn't end it, had no idea how to stop the downward spiral.

'Enrique?' said Santi.

Enrique swallowed hard. He was close to tears. 'It's . . . it's . . .'

'What? Come on, you can tell me? School? The academy? Are you homesick for Spain? Come on, Enrique, it can't be that bad.'

But it could. It was that bad and worse. Enrique wanted to blurt everything out, the whole story. But he was desperately scared that if he owned up to what he had done, his brother and everyone else would never forgive him.

It was too late for the truth.

'It's nothing, Santi,' he said at last.

'But there is something, I can see that for myself now.'

'Just a little homesick maybe. That's all. I'm fine.' He walked quickly towards the door. 'I need to get my bus. I'll be late.'

It was an academy training evening, and even though Enrique had largely avoided his three tormentors at school, his early morning conversation with his brother had been playing on his mind all day.

He couldn't get it out of his head that he was letting everyone down so badly. And that meant everyone here in England and everyone back home in Spain. His mother would never get over the shame and disgrace it would bring to the family if what he was doing came to light.

He couldn't let that happen, he couldn't be discovered. He just had to cope somehow, and hope that in time Jake and his friends would get bored with picking on him or turn their attentions elsewhere.

In the meantime, he had to make the best of school and try to improve at the academy. His form had dropped recently and he had noticed the looks of disappointment exchanged by the academy coaches.

He'd begun so well, but now it was falling to pieces, not just in matches but in training as well.

They were out on the pitch, working on skills in groups of five or six, with the coaches watching their every move and barking out instructions.

Enrique's group and another were playing a game of one-touch football. It was quick and exciting, just the sort thing that in normal times Enrique would have loved and excelled at.

But these were not normal times and Enrique was finding it almost impossible to concentrate on the game.

The two teams were on a vastly reduced playing area with markers at each end representing goalposts. The very tight space meant that it was all about controlled, accurate passing when the ball came to feet and searching for space when it was elsewhere.

Enrique had already mistimed a couple of passes, sending them to the opposition rather than to a team-mate, and he'd also dawdled when passes came his way, allowing them to be easily intercepted. Enrique's team were trailing on the goal tally, and Enrique knew it was mainly down to him.

The ball broke free and one of Enrique's team-mates pounced and sent a lovely pass directly towards him. But instead of going to meet it, Enrique waited again. An opponent nipped in just before it reached Enrique and his touch set up his team for another attack. Enrique snarled in frustration and instinctively grabbed the red training bib his opponent was wearing and yanked him back, causing him to fall heavily.

'Hey, what's that all about?' the boy shouted as play stopped and the other players stared.

'You . . . you . . .' Enrique knew he was completely in the wrong, but he was desperately searching for words to justify his reckless act.

'I took the ball off you, and you didn't like it. Is that what you're trying to say?' said the other boy, getting to his feet and rubbing his hip where he had fallen.'

'It was a mistake, I'm sorry . . .'

'Yeah, right!'

'*Enrique!*'

The academy director was striding towards him, and he looked furious. 'Go and get a shower. You're in another world tonight, and that's no good to me or anyone else here.'

'I'm sorry . . . I . . .'

'Just go. Now. We'll talk about it later.'

Enrique trudged away, head bowed. All around the training area young players glanced at each other and raised their eyebrows, wondering if maybe that was the last time Enrique would be out there with them.

Twenty-one

The Copa del Rey has been part of Spanish football for more than a hundred years. The competition has suffered in profile a little in recent years because of top club sides' obsession with their La Liga finishing position and Champions' League qualification, but it is still important. Players enjoy the cup matches, the fans love them, and for the winners there is a guaranteed place in the UEFA Cup.

And just like in England, the newspapers' sports editors and reporters look forward to the romance of the cup competitions because of the shocks and the upsets – especially when there is the chance that one of the minnows might knock out one of the giants after a David and Goliath type battle.

This season, Gavin Harris's Bardenas FC from Segunda B had been grabbing all the headlines with an incredible run through the competition. Now, at the last sixteen stage, with Bardenas drawn against mighty Real Madrid, the sports editors and reporters must have thought that Christmas had come early and that their greatest wish had been granted.

The tie had everything: the minnows against the millionaires, the country boys versus the city slickers, and to top it all off, the classic situation of a former Real Madrid superstar returning to the Bernabéu as both manager and supersub of the underdogs. Gavin was still making regular, albeit brief, appearances from the bench.

The back pages had been full of news and updates on the tie since the day the draw was made. Gavin had been interviewed by newspapers and magazines and had appeared on television and radio shows.

Camera crews and football reporters were suddenly visible in and around the stadium and all over the area, and it suddenly seemed that anyone with anything of even vague interest to say was appearing on television screens or in newspaper articles.

The match was over two legs, the first being at Bardenas with all 15,000 tickets sold out within hours of going on sale. The club had never before hosted a complete sell out – the players were accustomed to playing in front of a few thousand fans at best.

Now it was different. This was something new. For many of the team it would be something to tell their grandchildren about – their moment of football fame. And throughout the country, football followers were excited and intrigued by the pairing and fascinated to see how the tie would go.

Gavin was under no illusions; a shock victory was always possible in a one-off match, especially if the underdogs were at home and playing on a tight pitch with their partisan supporters close to the action.

That was possible, if unlikely, but over two legs – home and away, with Real at Bernabéu for the second leg – realistically there was virtually no chance of Bardenas progressing further in the competition.

But Gavin wasn't going to tell his players that. He'd been thinking for days about the content of his pre-match pep talk to the team. He wanted to send them out fired up but not overconfident, excited but not fearful. Most of all, he wanted them to enjoy what was likely to be one of the most memorable days of their lives.

They sat in the dressing room, changed and booted and ready to go. The noise and fervour of the crowd rang around the stadium and seemed to seep through the walls into the room.

Gavin, tracksuited and buzzing with nervous energy, prowled up and down. In his hand he held a copy of the Real Madrid team sheet. It read more or less how he had expected it to, but it gave him a little more ammunition to use in his pep talk. Real had left many of their big guns back in Madrid or on the bench. Gavin would have been surprised had it been otherwise: Real had a crunch league match approaching and they were still battling in the Champions League.

Now Gavin was going to use the opposition team selection to his advantage. 'So,' he said in Spanish, walking slowly up and down and making eye contact with each of his young players, smiling, nodding, attempting to banish their nerves, 'Real Madrid have decided they don't need to send their best players out against little Bardenas FC. Their second string will be good enough.'

He paused, letting the words sink in, shrugging his shoulders as he walked. 'We shall see, eh?' He smiled again and his players smiled back and nodded as they caught his eye.

Gavin's Spanish had improved immensely over the last year or so. It had been essential, as few of his squad knew more than a few words of English. 'Perhaps mighty Real Madrid have made a mistake.' He stopped, turned to his players, glared at them wide-eyed and roared, 'Am I right?'

The players instinctively yelled back, almost in unison, '*Si!*'

The sound must have reached to Real

Madrid's dressing room just across the corridor. It might almost have travelled back to the Bernabéu.

Gavin spoke softly this time, still in Spanish, knowing he needed to say little more. 'Enjoy it, all of you. This is your day.' He clenched both fists together and, this time in English, shouted at the top of his voice: 'Let's go!'

His players returned the compliment.

'*Yes!*'

Gavin Harris had always been a flair footballer, the type of player who could delight the fans one minute and frustrate them the next. He'd been accused of being lazy, of turning it on only when he wanted to and of going walkabout in matches he thought were unimportant.

There was probably an element of truth to all of that, but what was certain about Gavin was that on his day he had the skill and the vision to match the best and that he always wanted to play free-flowing, attacking football.

Nothing had changed now that Gavin was a manager. As a great goal-scorer it was only natural to him to put the emphasis on scoring goals, believing that if the opposition scored *three* goals then it was up to his team to score *four* – minimum.

It all made for exciting football, the type that was bringing steadily growing crowds to the new Bardenas stadium.

And the Bardenas team were playing just as their manager wanted. Gavin was prowling the touchline, close to the dugout, urging his players on, pointing, shouting, staring up to the heavens in disbelief every time a decision went against Bardenas.

The Real team were undoubtedly more skilful overall and were more comfortable on the ball. But Bardenas were putting in every bit of effort they could as they went for goal, sometimes leaving gaping holes at the back, which so far Real had failed to exploit.

And Bardenas had one added element to throw at Real – the blistering pace of Gavin's most recent signing, who was causing havoc and moments of sheer panic as he tore into and around the Real defence. The little winger's name was Ruben Casquero, and Gavin was convinced that the nineteen-year-old was destined for the big time.

He appeared to operate on long-life batteries because Gavin had discovered he could run all day. He was constantly beating his marker, and anyone else who got near him, and each time he went on a run the crowd roared their approval. His crosses were still erratic, but were getting better, and the Bardenas front men had twice almost got onto the end of one.

Real had also come close on a couple of occasions and the only surprise when the referee blew for half time was that there was no score. The players walked from the field to tumultuous applause and ringing cheers.

Gavin was in with his team and talking even before they'd sat down. He had words for every player; encouragement, advice. He was all movement and animation, telling them all that they were brilliant, even better than he'd expected and that the Real players couldn't believe what had hit them in the first forty-five minutes.

When Gavin came to Ruben Casquero, he sat

down next to him and spoke softly. 'Brilliant,' he said. 'Carry on the way you are and you'll be playing *for* Real next season, not against them.'

'But I like it here, boss,' said Ruben.

Gavin grinned as he replied and remembered. 'You'll like the Bernabéu even more.'

The second half picked up where the first had stopped. Excitement, attacks, goalmouth clearances, balls flying just wide of the uprights and just over the crossbar. Ruben Casquero was without doubt the Bardenas star player but their keeper was also performing heroics between the posts. He was the oldest player in the team, a veteran of twenty-eight, and he had played regularly at a much higher level. A long-term injury had blighted his career for a couple of years but in this match he was showing exactly how good he still was.

With twenty minutes remaining, the match was still somehow scoreless. Gavin had thought about putting himself on, but his team were playing so well he didn't really want to take anyone off and possibly affect the balance.

A few minutes later he had no choice. One of his front two fell awkwardly in an aerial challenge with a Real defender, and after trying to run off the knock for a couple of minutes he signalled to the bench that he had to come off.

Gavin had been warming up during those couple of minutes. He ran onto the pitch to ringing cheers, pointing and shouting to his team, letting them know exactly what he wanted as the match entered its final phase. Gavin knew his team were tired, exhausted. They might not have it in them to win the match, but after their magnificent effort he desperately wanted them not to lose it.

They hung on, with Gavin for once helping out in defence, operating in what was usually totally unexplored territory for him. But he wanted the draw – his team deserved it, they'd earned it.

The clock ticked down to a minute to go and there was likely to be no more than two additional minutes for stoppages. Still Real attacked, still Bardenas clung on, with Gavin making a goal line clearance from a ferocious shot from the edge of the box.

Ruben Casquero collected the ball and set off on a run out wide, with a Real midfielder giving chase and getting nowhere near the little winger.

Gavin took a huge breath and set off on a run of his own. He'd lost a yard of pace over the past few years but he knew he had to get up in support.

'Keep it wide,' he yelled to Ruben, thinking that they might just be able to keep the ball while the seconds ticked down to the final whistle. 'Hold onto it, just keep it.'

The Real defenders had grown accustomed to the danger of the winger. They too, wanted him out wide, out of the danger area. They would also be content with a draw now, knowing that the second leg would give them ample opportunity to take the tie.

Gavin was thundering up the centre as Ruben suddenly cut inside, leaving a defender completely wrong-footed. And then Gavin saw it: the goal was on, it was his for the taking. All it needed was the right delivery – into his path – and he wouldn't be able to miss. He couldn't.

'Give it,' he yelled to Ruben. 'Now, Ruben, *now*!'

The winger looked up, saw Gavin to his left and then hit the ball.

But not to Gavin.

He struck a thunderous shot, which kept low and beat the keeper at the near post, thudding into the net.

Gavin skidded to a standstill, eyes bulging, with the noise from the crowd sounding as though it was about to take the roof off the stands.

And then he shouted, '*Yes!* Yes, yes, *yes!*'

Twenty-two

Jamie, smiling as usual, stepped from his van and walked to the front door where Santi was waiting.

'Thanks for coming over, Jamie,' Santi said.

'No problem, mate, and you don't have to thank me. I finished a job this morning and there's no way I want to start another one this afternoon.'

Santi closed the door and they went through to the kitchen. 'Coffee?' he asked.

Jamie pulled a chair from beneath the kitchen table and nodded as he sat down. 'You been getting Gavin's texts?'

'I think the first one came about two minutes

after the match ended,' said Santi, laughing. 'He must still have been on the pitch. I reckon his cellphone bill must be more than he's earning right now.'

'What a result though! Pity there's got to be a second leg.'

Santi poured the coffee, brought the two mugs over to the table and sat opposite his friend. 'I think Real might have a slightly different team out next time.' He picked up a spoon and began to vigorously stir his coffee, although he had added neither milk nor sugar. Jamie could see he looked on edge.

'So, what's up then?' he asked. 'How's training going?'

'Up and down,' said Santi with a shrug. 'Had to sit it out a couple of days ago – foot started hurting again. Today it seems fine though.'

'Great. Follow me then.' Jamie pushed back his chair and stood up.

'What about your coffee?'

'Coffee can wait.'

Jamie went out to his van, with Santi following, and opened the back doors. The interior was packed with plumbing tools, welding gear, lengths of copper piping and even a couple of old cast-iron radiators. And sitting wedged between a radiator and a metal toolbox was a football. Jamie took it out. 'You allowed to have a gentle kick around?'

Santi laughed. 'That's just about what I do all the time.'

They went round to the back garden where there were long stretches of grass. Jamie dropped the ball onto his instep and juggled it from one foot to the other, onto his head and then back down to his feet.

'You always were good at that,' said Santi, nodding his appreciation.

Jamie was grinning, clearing enjoying himself. 'Better than you, Muñez, my man.'

'I'm not arguing.'

Jamie flicked the ball over to Santi, who brought it down to the ground and then passed it back. Soon they were playing with the enthusiasm of a couple of small schoolboys, and instead of Jamie and Santi kicking around in the back garden, they became

England versus Spain in the World Cup final at Wembley.

They made up the rules as they went along. Four trees became the goalposts, no tackling was allowed, and only two touches of the ball were permitted before the attacker had to take his shot.

England were leading 15–14 when Jamie called for a break. 'Half time!'

'No,' Santi protested. 'Just because you're winning you want a rest.'

Jamie started to laugh and Santi chuckled too, as they both realized they were not only playing like a couple of kids, they were acting like kids as well.

They sat side by side on a garden bench.

'Great game, eh?' said Santi.

'Best game in the world.'

Santi looked at his friend, remembering the time they spent together as raw youngsters at Newcastle. 'You still miss it?'

'Every day, Santi. Every day. At least I'm a pretty good plumber.'

'You were an even better footballer.'

'You haven't seen me welding pipes or fitting a new radiator,' said Jamie, smiling. The football was at his feet. He toe-poked it away, sending it speeding between two trees. 'And Jamie Drew scores again,' he said, doing his best to impersonate football commentator John Motson. 'That's sixteen–fourteen to England, a record score.'

'It's still half time,' Santi protested.

'I'll never *not* miss being a footballer, Santi,' Jamie said with a shrug of his shoulders. 'But I had to move on. I have a kick around with the lads at work, I watch you from the Gallowgate stand, but nothing will ever replace *playing* a proper game of football. I don't even mean at St James' in front of a capacity crowd. The reserves were great; nowadays a Sunday morning team would be great. But I can't do it, not if I want to be able to have a kick around in the garden with my son when he grows up.'

Santi nodded. 'Second half?'

'Keep working at it, Santi,' said Jamie as he stood up. 'Get over this injury and get out there on the pitch again. And when you do, you keep playing for as long as you can.' He walked between the two trees, rescued the ball from beneath a bush and punted it over to Santi. 'Your kick-off. First one to thirty's the winner.'

Twenty-three

The academy boss had given Enrique a final warning about his future behaviour and attitude. Enrique turned red with embarrassment as he was told that everyone had been more than impressed with him when he first arrived and it looked as though he could have a big future with the club. But now everything had changed, Enrique's play and training was not up to the required standard and his attitude was completely unacceptable.

There were no punches pulled and Enrique was told that normally, at this stage, a boy's parents or guardian would have been called in to discuss the situation. But as that was Santi, and he had enough to worry about in recovering from his injury, Enrique was going to get one more chance.

He left the office with the words *final warning* ringing in his ears. And at the next training session, as he took his place for a practice match, he was determined he was going to make a new start. No more mistakes, no bad attitude, total concentration, he told himself. He would put everything he could into turning in a good performance. Better than good, he was going to be brilliant.

But before kick-off there was something he had to do. Lining up with him in midfield was the boy he had dragged to the ground at the last training session.

Enrique trotted over to him, holding out his hand. 'I'm sorry about the other night, Joe,' he said. 'I don't know why I did it. Except . . . I wasn't feeling good.'

Joe smiled and shock Enrique's hand. 'Forget it.' He nodded towards the other team. 'Let's just stuff this lot, eh?'

'Yeah, we'll do that.'

Enrique trotted back to the centre midfield position feeling better than he had for a long time. He didn't know why, but the bullies had left him alone for a few days. His talk with the academy director had cleared the air. It really was time to make a new start and concentrate on what he was good at – football.

And from the kick-off, Enrique was back to his very best. Everyone – players on both sides, coaches, the academy director – noticed the change within a few minutes. Enrique was bossing the match again, a commanding and confident figure in the centre of midfield, like a different person to the reserved, hesitant and almost timid character he had become off the pitch.

He set up two goals in the first half in a totally dominant performance, and midway through the second period he netted one for himself with a rasping shot from all of twenty-five yards.

On the touchline the academy director shook his head and turned to one of the watching coaches. 'What is it with this kid? Playing like this he looks as though he could step up to the first team in a couple of years.'

When the match ended, Enrique left the field tired but elated. His midfield partner, Joe, came running up to him. 'Enrique?'

'Yes?' Enrique answered, fearing that perhaps the incident of the previous session had not after all, been forgotten. It hadn't, but not in the way Enrique feared; Joe was all smiles. 'Play like that every week and you can knock me over whenever you want!'

Enrique was reliving the match in his mind as he travelled home on the bus. He'd played well, he knew that, but there were things he'd got wrong. No one plays a perfect match, and as the bus trundled through the darkness, Enrique was analysing the few mistimed passes, the poor challenges, the wrong positioning.

Rather than dwell too much on the good moments, Enrique knew it was important to be critical, even when his overall performance had been outstanding. That was the way he would keep improving, and that was the way he was most likely to cement his place at the academy at the end of the season.

He was smiling as he stood up to get off the bus, remembering the perfectly timed shot that got his name on the score sheet. There was no point in being too critical; he had to enjoy the special moments too.

The bus came to a standstill and Enrique stepped off. But as the vehicle pulled away, Enrique's smile turned instantly into a look of dismay.

They were there: Jake, Jordan and Craig. They appeared from behind the bus shelter, the advertisements in the plastic panelling having hidden them from Enrique's vision as he got off the bus.

Jake was looking fed up and angry. 'Turned up at last then? You kept us waiting.'

'We don't like being kept waiting,' added Jordan.

'I've . . . I've been at the . . .'

'We know where you've been,' said Craig.

Enrique went to walk away, but his three classmates closed in on him.

'What do you want?' he asked.

'Want?' said Jake, deciding to smile. 'Why

should we want anything? We're mates, aren't we?'

Enrique said nothing. He just wanted to get home.

'Actually though,' Jake continued, 'there is something we want you to do. We're going for a little ride.'

'A . . . a ride? What do you mean?'

'A drive.' Jake lifted both hands and mimed holding a car's steering wheel. 'We're going for a little ride around town.'

Craig nodded. 'And being as you're so good at starting cars, we need your help.'

'No,' said Enrique quickly. 'I won't do that, not again.'

'Oh, but you will, Enrique,' said Jake with a smile. 'We've got a video that says you will.'

'Aye,' added the grinning Jordan. 'And we're very sorry, we couldn't find you a Lamborghini this time; not many of them around the town. But we have got you a nice Jaguar.'

'Beautiful car,' said Jake. 'Speed and luxury; seats four perfectly. You'll love it.'

* * *

The gunmetal-grey, sleek Jaguar was parked in a quiet side street lined with office buildings, all of them in total darkness.

Enrique stood in the shadows with Jake and the others about forty metres from the vehicle. 'What if the driver comes back?'

Jake shook his head. 'We've checked it out more than once. Whoever owns it must live around here, somewhere there's nowhere to park.'

'Or maybe works here,' added Craig. 'Pub or a club.'

'Whatever,' said Jake. 'But no one's ever turned up, not when we've been watching.'

'But that doesn't mean no one will come tonight,' said Enrique. 'And the car . . . there may be an alarm.'

Jake grabbed Enrique's jacket collar with both hands and pulled him close. 'That's a risk we'll take then,' he hissed. 'It's what makes it interesting. Let's get on with it.'

There was to be nothing subtle about the method of entry into the vehicle. As they walked across the street, Jordan pulled a short crowbar from inside his zipped-up bomber jacket. They reached the Jaguar and Jordan took the end of the crowbar in his right hand, pulled his arm back and smashed the heavy, handle end of the bar against the side window. There was a loud cracking sound but the glass held firm.

'Hit the thing,' Jake ordered. 'Harder!'

Jordan drew his arm back, turned his head away and thumped the crowbar into the window for a second time. This time the glass shattered, spraying shards and splinters into the vehicle and onto the road. But no alarm sounded.

Jake laughed. 'Some people deserve to have their cars taken.' He quickly got into the vehicle and found the bonnet release catch. 'Over to you, mister expert,' he said to Enrique as the bonnet sprang free.

Enrique hesitated for a moment, but only for a moment, because Jordan was standing at his side, the crowbar raised and ready to put a stop to any protests. As Craig held up the bonnet, Enrique went to work, while Jake brushed away the broken glass inside the vehicle and Jordan stood watching for unwanted passers-by.

Within a minute, the engine purred into life. Jake was already behind the wheel. As Enrique stepped back, Craig dropped the bonnet shut.

'Here we go,' shouted Jake, dropping into broad Geordie as he revved the powerful engine. 'H'way, the lads!'

Twenty-four

Roz was on one of her rare late shifts at the hospital. It wasn't her favourite part of the job, but it worked OK when Santi was at home to look after Rosie. When he wasn't, Rosie stayed at Lorraine's for the night, which she loved.

Roz was a sister on the Intensive Care ward. It was an important job, part of an expert and dedicated team. They had to be – one wrong action could be critical, the difference between life and death because every patient on the ward was dangerously ill or had been seriously injured.

So it was a difficult and complex job, and the ward was almost always busy. Tonight was no exception.

Roz was tired; it had been a long and exhausting shift with several patients needing sudden urgent treatment and others constant monitoring. Roz didn't talk much about her work, not even to Santi. Often the ward staff didn't even talk to each other about the things they saw or had to cope with during their shift. It could be too difficult to speak about it, even when the crisis was over, one way or the other.

Roz was in her small office, writing up notes and trying to find the time to drink a mug of tea, when the telephone rang. She sighed as she reached for the phone and picked it up; the ringing rarely signalled good news. 'Hello.'

It was the Accident and Emergency department sister. 'Roz, there'll be two young lads coming up soon, RTA. There's another not so bad who's going into a general ward and there's a fourth still in theatre. We're not sure if he's going to make it.'

'OK, thanks, Jenny,' answered Roz, calmly. 'We'll be ready.'

They were always ready. They had to be; there was no other choice. And road traffic accidents were common enough for her to know what kind of injuries to expect. She put down the telephone and reached for her mug of tea. It seemed hours since she'd eaten or drunk anything and she was desperately thirsty. She took a sip and then screwed up her face and shuddered as she swallowed.

The tea was stone cold.

It was very late when Roz finally arrived home. She'd telephoned Santi when she got the chance so she knew he would be waiting up.

She parked her car in the driveway, wearily climbed out and went to the front door, where Santi was standing. He saw instantly that Roz looked pale and completely drained.

She forced a limp smile as Santi kissed her on the cheek and helped her off with her coat.

'Is Rosie OK?' she asked.

'Fine. Haven't heard a thing since I put her to bed.'

Roz kicked off her shoes, staggered through to the living room and slumped down onto a sofa. She wasn't much of an alcohol drinker, but she smiled gratefully when Santi sat next to her and gave her a small glass of brandy. She sipped the liquid and felt the warm, almost burning sensation as it slid down her throat.

Tonight, for once, she needed to talk. 'They stole a car; drove through the city at stupid speed and the police followed them. They didn't even chase them, just kept them in view and called more vehicles in. But they still went faster and faster.'

She put her head back on the sofa and closed her eyes for a moment, remembering what had happened when the injured youngsters had been brought in to the ward.

Opening her eyes, because sometimes it was best not to think for too long, she took another small sip of the brandy. 'Apparently the car went round a corner and there was another kid crossing the road. They hit him, knocked him up into the air and then the car smashed into a wall.'

Roz fell silent and Santi took the brandy glass, which was almost slipping from her hand. He leaned forward and placed the glass on the coffee table.

As he sat back they heard a movement in the doorway. They both turned and looked back; Enrique was standing there.

'Enrique,' Santi said. 'I thought you were asleep. How long have you been standing there?'

Enrique was ashen-faced and staring at Roz. 'The car . . . what was it?'

'What?' said Roz, confused.

'What sort of car? The make?'

'How should I know? I didn't see the car.'

'The boys then, what were their names?'

Santi stood up. 'Why do you want to know this, Enrique?'

Enrique moved into the room, close to Roz. 'Please, Roz, tell me? Their names?'

'I . . . I don't know the name of the one who was hit by the car. He was still in theatre when I left. But the two who came to the ward . . . one was Jordan and the other was . . . Jake. There was another boy; he went to a general ward, so I don't—'

'Craig,' said Enrique, his voice almost a whisper. 'It was Craig.'

Roz's eyes widened. 'How do you know that?'

Enrique looked as though his legs were about to give way. He sank down onto a chair.

'What's going on?' demanded Santi. 'Enrique, how do you know this boy's name?'

Enrique gazed up at his brother, tears in his eyes. 'They made me start the car. Hotwire it, they knew I could do it. I thought they would take me with them, but they pushed me away and drove off. I said I wouldn't help them, but they made me, Santi. They *made* me.'

Twenty-five

The interview room was cold and starkly furnished. Enrique sat in silence, Santi at his side. He'd told the whole story, from beginning to end, to the listening police officers.

The detective sergeant shook his head and closed his notebook. 'What I still don't understand,' he said looking at Enrique, 'is why you never reported the bullying. We know the school, they're very good at dealing with this sort of thing; that's why bullying hardly ever happens there.'

Enrique shrugged his shoulders. He didn't know what to say any more; he'd explained as best he could.

They had been at the police station for hours. As soon as Santi and Roz had said they had to report exactly what had happened, Enrique had nodded his agreement. There had been no argument and no attempt to save his own skin.

As he told the police every detail of what had happened in the run-up to stealing the Jaguar, Enrique didn't like what he was hearing about himself. He came over as weak and feeble, like someone else, not the boy he had been in Madrid. He didn't know why; all he knew was that any excuse he tried to make would only be lame and unconvincing.

He felt ashamed; he had let down himself and his family.

But Santi wasn't going to let down his young brother. He and Enrique had talked together that night like they'd never talked before, and he'd learned how Enrique had got so much terribly wrong since arriving in Newcastle – and why. Now Santi was going to stand by him. He felt like *he* had let *Enrique* down, not the other way round. 'He wanted to fit in,' he said to the police officer. 'And it was all new to him, and different;

the school, the football academy, everything. He wanted to be accepted, it wasn't easy. And I . . . I was too busy to notice.'

The police officer didn't look convinced. 'There are a lot of young people in exactly the same position these days, Mr Muñez. It's fortunate for us, and for them, that they don't all get themselves into situations like this.'

'But—'

'No, Santi,' said Enrique, interrupting, 'he's right; I should never have let it get to this. I tried to . . . to be big, to boast . . . about you, my life in Madrid, everything. I tried to . . . to win their friendship, instead of just being me.'

Now that Enrique was finally facing up to exactly where he'd gone wrong he found he still had more to say. 'When they started the bullying I wanted to show them I was strong . . . tough . . . that it didn't bother me. But it did. And then they made the video.'

The detective sergeant nodded. 'Yes, we found the phone in the wreckage of the car.' He shook his head. 'Hardly the crime of the century, was it?' he said to Enrique. 'If you really had wanted to show some strength you'd have reported what was going on; to the school or to your brother.' He smiled, very slightly, for the first time. 'Or even to us.'

'Yes,' said Enrique nodding. 'Yes, I know that now.'

The door opened and a uniformed officer looked in and spoke to the sergeant. 'Could I have a word, sarge?'

The sergeant got up and went out of the room. Within a minute he was back. This time he didn't sit down. 'We just heard from the hospital. The young man hit by the vehicle is going to pull through, and so are your . . . friends. Let's hope when they get out of hospital they'll learn from this as well.'

'So what happens now?' asked Santi. 'To Enrique?'

'That depends, Mr Muñez.'

'Depends? On what?'

The police officer gathered up his notes. 'On a number of things.'

Twenty-six

One of England's greatest ever strikers, the legendary goal-poacher Jimmy Greaves, turned to television punditry after he retired as a player and soon came up with what was to become a famous catchphrase: 'Football's a funny old game.'

Gavin Harris was thinking exactly that as he sat alone in the visitors' dressing room at the Bernabéu Stadium before the start of the second leg of the Copa del Rey quarterfinal. His team, the substitutes and his two assistants were out on the pitch for the warm-up. Gavin had sent them out, telling them he'd join them soon.

But for a few moments he wanted to sit alone,

and remember. He was back, back at the stadium where he'd enjoyed some of his greatest moments in football. He didn't even realize he was smiling as he thought about the great matches, the dressing-room banter, the world-class footballers he'd played alongside and against. Zidane, Ronaldo, Roberto Carlos, Raúl, David Beckham and of course, Santiago Muñez, they had all been team-mates, while other superstars of football like Ronaldinho and Thierry Henry had been amongst his illustrious opponents.

Gavin had loved being part of what was universally thought of as the greatest club in the world. But that was in the past and as he sat there thinking, he knew he was happy now that it was. He'd moved on and was perfectly content as player-manager of the Segunda B outfit, Bardenas FC.

Gavin's young and enthusiastic team had upset the odds and all the predictions with their narrow first leg victory at their home stadium, proving yet again that football really was a funny old game.

But with many of the Real Madrid big guns

back in the starting line-up this time, the outcome was likely to be very different. In some ways Gavin hoped it would be. His team had suffered one of those 'cup success backlashes' in the league game following the victory over Real, losing three–nil to a team they should have beaten.

The defeat was a blow to the push for promotion and Gavin was admitting, to himself at least, that the cup run had probably gone as far as it should, let alone could. But he was determined that his players would enjoy the experience, and that he would too. After all, it might be some time before his next visit to the home of Real Madrid in any other capacity than that of spectator.

He glanced again at the Real team sheet and smiled. It was a multi-million line-up in any currency – euros, pounds or dollars. His own squad had cost next to nothing, and that made him even more proud of what they'd achieved together.

Gavin felt his cellphone vibrate in his tracksuit top pocket. He'd been waiting for this, and as he pushed open the phone he saw that it was the text he'd expected, from Santi:

Good luck m8. Score 1 4 me!

Gavin laughed. 'I'll do my best, mate.'

He shut down the phone, opened the door of his locker and slipped it inside. He was about to join his players out on the pitch when the door to the dressing room opened and the entire squad and the coaches started to troop in. The time had flown by; Gavin had entirely missed the warm-up.

It didn't matter and Gavin didn't care, because a few minutes later he was standing on the marble staircase leading down to the players' tunnel to the pitch, ready to lead his team out for the real thing, the match. The Real players and their management team were on one side of the staircase divide and Gavin and his team on the other.

There were a few nods and waves and thumbs up from old team-mates, and then everyone began to clatter down the stairs, their studs making a familiar echoing sound that brought back even more memories for Gavin.

As they emerged from the canvas awning covering the final part of the tunnel, Gavin saw that many of the *Madridistas*, the Real fans, were getting to their feet and applauding. That wasn't unusual – most supporters stand to cheer and welcome their team onto the pitch – but then Gavin heard his name being chanted: the *Madridistas* were welcoming back one of their own, one of the victors of their Champions League winning team.

Gavin strode on, smiling from ear to ear, waving with both arms raised to every corner of the massive ground, and the noise level increased from every side.

The next minutes passed quickly – with team photos and handshakes – and then Gavin was sitting on the bench and the match was underway.

The Bardenas youngsters seemed to have forgotten the misery of their league defeat and were picking up where they'd left off in the first leg, pressing and attacking with urgency and no little skill.

But this time they were up against a far more

experienced Real Madrid team, a team that weren't going to panic when a goal didn't come in the first twenty minutes. They absorbed the pressure and looked comfortable, although Real came no closer to scoring than Bardenas had.

At half time, though there was still no score, and although Real didn't look rattled, there were a few whistles from the *Madridistas* accompanying the shrill blast of the ref's whistle when it sounded to bring the first period to a close.

Gavin felt nothing but pride for his players as they trooped off the pitch, but he also noticed that several were looking extremely tired, having given their all for the team. He would have to make careful use of his substitutes to get the team through the match.

When they returned for the second half, Real had made a couple of substitutions of their own. Bardenas were now facing a virtually full-strength Real Madrid.

Gavin made changes and still Bardenas held on. It seemed that a miracle might just be on the cards.

Until the seventy-sixth minute.

Little Bardenas winger, Ruben Casquero, who had virtually run himself into the ground, was for once beaten to the ball. It moved swiftly upfield and the Bardenas midfielders fell back, looking to protect their defence.

But one of the Real substitutes, Gonzalo Higuain, the idol of the *Madridistas*, came storming through the middle and hit a blistering, unstoppable shot which screamed into the top of the net.

Gavin saw his players visibly sag; most were exhausted, just not used to football at this pace and level. But the last thing Gavin wanted for his brave team was the humiliation of a flood of goals against them in the closing stages of the match.

Real still needed to win the tie, and a minute later they were two up and finally ahead on aggregate. The scrappy goal came through a combination of a defensive mix up in the penalty box and weary Bardenas legs.

Gavin put himself on, to ringing cheers from the *Madridistas*. He slotted in to a defensive central position, looking to stiffen the midfield.

But defence had never been one of Gavin's specialities and with eighty-six minutes on the clock, Real netted their third.

This wasn't the way Gavin wanted to depart the Bernabéu for the last time. He swore under his breath and moved up to the front for the restart, grabbing a word with Ruben Casquero as the ball was placed on the centre spot.

When the whistle sounded Ruben ran out wide and deep. Gavin received the ball from his centre forward, but rather than playing the quick pass he moved back, watching Ruben's run and skilfully avoiding a fairly half-hearted tackle from a Real midfielder. Real knew the match was won now, there was no point in over-exerting themselves today with a hectic finale to the season still to come.

Looking up, Gavin struck a perfectly weighted, thirty-five yard crossfield pass that rolled back the years and fell invitingly at the feet of Ruben Casquero. He ran on with the ball as Gavin sprinted, a lot slower than he had in his prime, up the centre, looking for the ball which he hoped would arrive in the box.

But Ruben was still not the finished article. The run was good, beating the full back was good, but the delivery of the final ball was terrible. Instead of flying at pace high across the centre of the box where Gavin was lurking, it stayed low and bounced out towards two Real defenders. For some inexplicable reason – perhaps the presence of wily old goal-poacher Gavin Harris – they both went to make the clearance. They simply got in each other's way, misread the bounce and sent the ball spinning towards a startled Gavin.

He didn't even have time to react – he just stared as the ball struck his knee and bobbled past a completely wrong-footed Iker Casillas and into the net.

The *Madridistas* roared their approval and Gavin stood there laughing as his players crowded in to congratulate him. He'd done it, scored again at the Bernabéu. It was probably the luckiest, flukiest goal he had ever scored, but he'd done it, the evidence was nestling there in the back of the net.

Even Casillas was smiling as he shook his

head and scooped to collect the ball.

And Gavin could hardly wait to read the text from Santi, which he knew would be on his phone when he got back to the dressing room.

Twenty-seven

There had been meetings at school and meetings at the academy. There had been discussions with teachers, coaches and police officers. Santi had been at Enrique's side for every moment. He knew he'd been preoccupied with his own affairs; now he was putting Enrique first.

Even before the meetings he'd spoken for hours on the phone to his mother in Spain. And so had Enrique. Rosa-Maria wanted to come over to England to be there for her youngest son, but Santi had urged her to wait until the outcome of the meetings and discussions was known.

Now it was, and decisions had been made. The police were not going to prosecute Enrique.

He had been formally warned and cautioned about future behaviour, but he was to be allowed to remain in school and to stay on at the academy.

School and academy both agreed that there was no point in issuing further final warnings. Enrique knew the score only too well; if he wanted a future in England he had to impress in every area. And quickly, for time was running out.

Jake and Jordan, along with their roadcrash victim, were still in hospital. Once they were able to go home, Jake and Jordan would be facing a number of charges, along with Craig, who had been released from hospital but had not returned to school.

So for Enrique, the long nightmare was over and it was entirely down to him to ensure that it didn't return. Santi was driving him back from the academy when he brought up the issue that was on both their minds. 'What about Mama, do you want her to come over?'

Enrique shook his head. 'Not now. If that's OK with you and Roz?'

'But why not? You know she wants to help.'

'Everyone wants to help,' said Enrique. 'And everyone has. And if Mama comes now, we'll have to go over it all again and again. I want to move on, Santi, I really do. I'll see Mama at the end of the season like we always planned.'

Santi nodded; he could understand exactly what his brother was thinking. 'OK, I'll speak to her tonight, and—'

'No,' Enrique said quickly. 'I'll speak to her. Explain. And I want to tell her how you and Roz have helped me get through this.'

It was true enough. Since they had found out what had been going on, both Santi and Roz had done everything they could to support Enrique.

'And don't forget Rosie,' said Santi with a smile. 'You know you can never leave her out.'

'Oh, I know that,' laughed Enrique. 'Rosie makes certain she's never forgotten.'

The car came to a junction and Santi waited for the traffic flow to pass. 'We all make mistakes, Enrique. I made some pretty bad ones myself when I was a lot older than you are now.' They drove in silence for a few minutes, but as they got closer to home Santi was conscious that Enrique still had something on his mind. 'What is it?' he asked.

Enrique hesitated for a moment. 'It's . . . it's you. You helped me so much and . . . and we never spoke about you. Your injury, I didn't even ask how it is. Or your treatment, or training. I know you missed some sessions because of me.'

Santi shrugged. 'I'm doing all right, getting there.'

'But the World Cup is so important to you.'

'Yeah, and so is my family. Sometimes we have to change priorities.'

'But if you miss the World Cup because of me . . .'

'I won't miss the World Cup because of you. If I miss it, it'll be because I'm not ready.'

They were back. Santi turned the vehicle in at the driveway and pulled the car to a standstill and turned off the engine. Enrique opened the door and went to get out.

'Enrique?'

Enrique looked back. 'Yeah?'

Santi smiled. 'I *will* be ready.'

Twenty-eight

The domestic season moved swiftly on to its conclusion. At times it seemed that Santi's confident prediction that he would be ready for the World Cup looked to be spot on, at other times it appeared to be wildly optimistic.

Newcastle United's season ended with Premiership respectability, if not the silverware players, management and supporters yearned for. Santi, far from featuring heavily in the closing stages of the campaign, made just two appearances, both from the bench and both fairly brief.

The first was little more than a runout, testing the foot in match conditions. Santi was tentative throughout the cameo appearance and came off at the final whistle with his foot aching and feeling more than a bit downhearted. But the doctors and coaches said the aching was to be expected at this stage; the important point was that the foot and the metatarsal bone appeared to be fine.

It gave Santi the confidence to be more ambitious in his second appearance. He realized that there was no point in hanging back; there were no easy rides in the Premiership, and it would be even harder should he make the World Cup finals, which were by now just a few weeks away.

He threw himself into the final twenty minutes of the match with a level of commitment and enthusiasm that had coaches and supporters alike wincing with concern and fearing the worse. Everyone had seen comebacks that ended in disaster.

But the big effort paid off in spectacular style when Santi scored a fantastic goal, a trademark right-footed volley from all of thirty-five yards after a flat out run to receive the pass. It was Santiago Muñez at his outstanding best, and although it guaranteed nothing, it was more than enough to grab the back page headlines the following day, and enough also to remind the Spanish coach that Santi was back.

Across the globe, footballers from thirty-two nations waited anxiously to know if they would be travelling to South Africa for the greatest tournament in world football. Some were nailed-on certainties to be there, others could only wait and hope. Santi was in the latter group.

In Spain, Bardenas FC's and Gavin's season ended in 'so near yet so far' disappointment. After the second Real Madrid match, the team rallied to finish top of their Segunda Division B group. It was a fantastic achievement, but the complex Spanish promotion system meant that they still had to battle out a sixteen-team play-off to determine which four teams would gain promotion to the country's second-tier league.

It had been a gruelling and exhausting season for Bardenas and the play-offs proved to be one step too far. But Gavin Harris had made his mark as both a coach and a manager, and as he prepared to fly out to South Africa to take up his

World Cup television job, he had high hopes and big plans for his managerial future.

Enrique also had a dramatic end to his football season. He'd knuckled down and put in a huge effort at the academy. And his efforts were rewarded when he was offered a full academy place for the following season.

It was everything he'd dreamed of when he'd first arrived in England, but surprisingly, to Santi at least, he asked for a little time to think it over before making his decision.

Santi was baffled, but Roz urged him not to press Enrique into giving his answer until he was ready.

'But I don't understand it,' Santi said. 'It's exactly what he wanted, the start of a career in football. What is there to think about?'

'There's a huge amount for him to think about, Santi,' Roz answered. 'He's had a difficult time, and even though he's come through it, if he says yes it means committing to being here in England for some time, for years.'

'But that's what he wanted.'

'Yes, and that was before he knew what the

reality of living in a different country would really be like.'

Santi thought about what Roz had said for a few moments and then he nodded. 'Yeah, you're right. It's good that he thinks about it for a little while before he tells them he's staying.'

'Yes, thank you. Thank you very much. Yes, goodbye. And thank you. Very much.'

Santi looked at the hand holding the cellphone – *his* hand. It was trembling. Then he realized that it wasn't just his hand, he was trembling all over, from head to toe. He took a couple of deep breaths, then finally remembered to shut down his phone. He stared out through the window to the garden. It was a beautiful morning, bright and cloudless. Roz was out there with Rosie and Enrique.

'Calm,' said Santi quietly to himself. He took another deep breath. 'Stay calm. Relaxed. Easy.'

His heart was thumping – he could hear it – but he opened the back door and walked slowly down the garden, trying to look relaxed and cool.

Roz was on her knees in a flowerbed, digging

out weeds that had sprung up between the early flowers. Enrique was helping her and Rosie was helping Enrique, although 'helping' had a different meaning as far as Rosie was concerned. She hadn't quite grasped the difference between weeds and flowers and was enthusiastically trying to wrench out of the ground every plant she could get her hands on. Enrique was doing his best to explain the difference between weeds and flowers without much success, especially as Rosie told him lots of the weeds were flowers.

Roz glanced up as she heard Santi coming down the garden and noticed immediately the strained look on his face. 'What's wrong?' she asked.

'Nothing,' said Santi, his voice husky with the tension of trying to stay calm. 'Why should there be something wrong?'

'I dunno,' Roz said with a shrug. 'You look . . . funny. Doesn't he, Enrique?'

Enrique took a few moments to decide but then he nodded. 'Yeah. Kind of . . . weird.'

'Weird?' said Santi, offended. 'I do not look weird. Or funny!'

'Daddy's funny,' Rosie added as she made a grab for another perfectly healthy plant, which Enrique just about managed to prevent her from uprooting.

'Well, you look, different then,' said Roz. 'What is it?'

'I . . . I . . .'

'Come on, Santi, spit it out, the weeds will have taken over the garden if you don't get on with it.'

Santi had done his best to stay calm, he'd made it through the back door and all the way down the garden without shouting or yelling, but now he couldn't hold back any longer. He raised both arms above his head, threw his head back and shouted at the top of his voice: 'I'm *in*! I am *in*! Muñez makes the Spanish World Cup squad!'

The yells were loud enough to stop even Rosie's quest to destroy every living thing in the flowerbed. 'Daddy *is* funny,' she said to Roz, looking completely bewildered.

'He certainly is, darling,' answered Roz as she got to her feet and went to hug the beaming Santi. 'I'm so happy for you,' she said, holding him tightly. 'You really deserve it after all you've been through this season.'

Santi could hardly contain his delight. When Enrique walked over, his hand held out to shake Santi's, his big brother just brushed it away and hugged him too. Then Rosie tottered over, not wanting to be left out, and it became an everyone hugging everyone else situation.

'It's only the squad,' said Santi when Rosie finally decided she'd had enough hugging. 'I've got to prove my fitness, but there's time. The important thing is, I'm going, I'm going to South Africa!'

Santi was still buzzing later in the day when he sat in the kitchen with Roz. Rosie was upstairs having an afternoon nap, so they were taking the opportunity to talk through the arrangements they would need to make now that the World Cup finals were part of their plans.

They hadn't got far in the discussions when Enrique came into the room. Santi was still all smiles. 'You OK, bro?'

Enrique nodded. 'There's something I need to tell you both.'

'More good news,' said Santi to Roz, assuming his brother was finally going to confirm his acceptance of the academy place.

'I wanted to wait until you knew about the World Cup squad,' said Enrique.

'That's kind of you, bro, but you didn't have to wait. We'll make it a double celebration anyway.'

'I don't know about celebration,' said Enrique, 'not when you hear what I have to say.' Santi's smile disappeared as Enrique continued quickly. 'I'm not going to take the place at the academy. I want to go home to Spain.'

'But . . . but you've been doing so well at the academy,' said Santi. 'Everyone's told me. They say you've been brilliant; they want you to stay on. And school, you've done well there too. Made new friends as well.'

'Yes,' said Enrique. 'I've worked hard to do good, for you and Roz. To thank you for everything you've done for me when I let you down so badly. I didn't want to leave as a failure at the academy or at school.'

'Then why go now? We got through the

tough times and you'll be giving up such an opportunity.'

'Yes, I know. But I think I have to make a new start. Maybe a club in Spain will take me. I hope so.'

'You'll have to prove yourself all over again.' Santi was desperately trying to convince his brother to stay. 'And maybe the Spanish clubs won't like it that you walked away from a club here.'

Enrique shrugged his shoulders. 'I'll have to take that chance.'

'You know we'll support whatever decision you make, Enrique, but are you certain about this?' asked Roz gently. 'Certain you're doing the right thing?'

'No, I'm not certain,' said Enrique, 'but I think it's what I must do. I'll wait until school ends, and then I'll go home.'

Twenty-nine

World Cup fever had struck South Africa, although the tournament itself was still more than a fortnight away.

Ever since the draw for the groupings had been made in Cape Town back in December, the excitement had been building, and now that the finals were approaching and the national squads were moving into their training camps, that excitement was reaching fever pitch.

Traditionally, sporting South Africa was all about top-level rugby union and cricket, with the Springboks current holders of the William Webb Ellis Cup, the official title of the Rugby World Cup, having beaten England in the final in Paris in October 2007. And South Africa were also the winners when the competition was held on home turf back in 1995.

But football was the growing game in every corner of the Rainbow Nation. Five brand-new stadiums had been built for the forthcoming tournament, while five more had been totally modernized and refurbished. Every effort was being put into the first-ever football World Cup finals to be staged on African soil, and the organizers knew that not only would thousands upon thousands of football fans from all over the world arrive to support their teams, there would also be a global TV audience of more than eleven billion people.

The presence of the host nation in the finals was also providing a huge boost to domestic football throughout the country. The Kaizer Chiefs, SuperSport United, Bloemfontain Celtic and Mamelodi Sundowns, amongst many others, were not yet household names in the footballing world but they were huge attractions in South Africa itself, drawing ever-increasing crowds.

Globetrotting South African players who had

plied their trade in the European leagues for many years were returning to their home country to play and exciting young talents were also featuring heavily in the domestic leagues.

And the country also had its very own budding Roman Abramovich in Patrice Motsepe, a mining magnate and one of the world's richest men, who owned Mamelodi Sundowns and was ploughing huge amounts of his money into the club.

The domestic game was in great shape and it could only get better with the World Cup finals being played in the country. The fantastic new stadiums, some of which had been in operation for the previous year's Confederations Cup, would be an ongoing legacy from the tournament, and the presence of the world's greatest players would raise the profile of football to unprecedented heights throughout the nation.

And as the thirty-two squads arrived in the country and set up their training bases close to the location of their group matches, expectations that this would be one of the best ever World Cup tournaments were running high.

Santi and the rest of the Spanish squad had settled in at their training camp and quickly became accustomed to the daily routine of training, followed by relaxation and treatment periods and then the obligatory press conferences and media interviews.

Santi was delighted to be there but he had left England with much still on his mind. Just before joining the rest of the squad for the journey to South Africa he had another long conversation with Enrique, trying once more to get him to change his mind about leaving Newcastle.

But Enrique could be just as stubborn as his big brother; all he would commit to was finishing the school year and remaining in England until Santi returned from the World Cup.

There was nothing more Santi could do or say to change his mind; from then on he had to be completely focused on getting match fit and trying to win a place in the Spanish team. It wasn't going to be easy – Spain already had two of the world's leading strikers in Fernando Torres and David Villa and they were both in terrific form.

Training was going well for the whole

squad, and after the European Championships success and the World Cup qualification campaign, Spain were amongst the favourites to lift the trophy.

Santi's broken metatarsal had completely healed, but he was still being assessed and monitored and receiving regular massage.

He was lying on a treatment table when the Spanish squad's press officer looked in. 'Santi, you haven't forgotten your television interview, have you?'

Santi looked up. 'Interview? I don't have any interviews today.'

'It's been arranged for days,' said the press officer with a sigh of exasperation. 'I told you, you must remember. The television team are ready in the press room. Don't keep this interviewer waiting, Santi, he's not the sort of guy we should upset.'

The press officer disappeared and Santi hauled himself upright, slid off the table and found his trainers. 'I don't remember any interview being booked,' he moaned as he slid his feet into the trainers.

He made his way through the building to the press room, pushed open the doors and went inside. The camera and sound technicians were setting up and checking equipment, but there was no sign of any interviewer.

'Er, hello,' said Santi to the technicians, 'I'm Santiago Muñez. I think someone's waiting to interview me.'

'*Was* waiting,' said the cameraman. 'But he got fed up waiting so he's gone for a coffee.'

'He's *what*?'

The cameraman shrugged. 'He's a bit of a temperamental artiste.'

'Yeah, sounds it,' said Santi, flopping down on a chair and stopping himself from saying what he was thinking. He didn't want to play the prima donna but some of these TV guys thought they owned the players and could say and do what-ever they wanted.

He sat there for a full five minutes, getting more and more agitated. He was just about to leave when the door behind him opened. He turned and saw a very familiar figure smiling at him. 'Kept you waiting, did I, mate?'

The press officer was also there. He was laughing and so were the two television technicians.

Santi stood up, all smiles. 'I should have guessed it would be you? How ya doing, Gav?'

Thirty

Santi had always been a favourite target of Gavin's practical jokes – once when they'd been riding in a lift from a hotel sauna to their rooms, dressed in nothing but large white towels, he'd managed to whip away Santi's towel and push him, stark naked, into the packed hotel reception area – but there was also a serious side to this visit.

Gavin really was on an interview mission. All the TV companies, including the one Gavin was working for, were looking for interesting feature programmes as part of the build-up to the World Cup.

And Gavin, as a former player and known and

liked by most of the top world stars, had come up with a programme concept of his own. He was talking to top players from every nation and getting them to talk about *their* favourite players in their own position. Strikers were talking about strikers, midfielders about midfielders, and so on. And after each interview, the TV company researchers were hunting out archive footage to back up and highlight the comments made by the interviewed player.

The first few features had already been broadcast and were proving a big success, with Gavin being praised as a television natural.

Now it was Santi's turn to sit in the hot seat and give his views on some of the other strikers featuring at the World Cup, even though Gavin's surprise arrival had given him little time to prepare.

But as the cameras began to roll, Santi had no problem in coming up with the names of strikers he admired and the reasons why.

He mentioned Lionel Messi of Argentina, Arsenal's Mexican wonderkid, Carlos Vela, Wayne Rooney of England and one or two more superstars of the world footballing stage.

But when it came down to it, Santi knew exactly who his two favourite strikers were. 'Fernando Torres and David Villa,' he said as the camera continued to roll.

'But they're your two main rivals for a starting place in the Spanish team,' Gavin replied.

'Don't I know it,' agreed Santi, nodding and smiling. 'But you asked me who my favourite strikers are, it's them.'

He went on to describe the outstanding qualities of the two strikers, their skills, positioning, pace, power, strength. He was full of praise and totally honest and it made for a terrific interview.

When it was all over and the crew had packed up and gone, Gavin stayed on. It was the first chance he'd had to speak face to face to Santi for quite a while and there was a lot to catching up to get through. It was winter in South Africa, but they strolled out in warm sunshine into the grounds surrounding the training complex.

'You're pretty good at this TV game,' Santi said. 'Could be a whole new career there if you want it.'

'Yeah, but it's not the same as being really involved in football,' answered Gavin. 'I mean, properly, day to day. Out there on the pitch.'

'And what about managing?'

'It's great,' said Gavin with a smile. 'So far, anyway. Maybe it won't be so great when results are not so good, but at the moment I'm loving it. Though it can never be like playing.'

'But you *are* still playing.'

'Just about,' laughed Gavin. 'Fifteen minutes, twenty max. Next season I think I'll have to make way for one of the younger kids. Have to give youth its chance.'

They walked on and eventually sat on a bench beneath of one of the huge trees in the grounds.

Gavin could see that Santi was deep in thought. 'Is that what's worrying you?' he said. 'After all the work and effort you've put in to get over your injury, you'll just get fifteen or maybe twenty minutes to show what you can do?'

Santi shrugged but didn't answer.

Gavin sat back on the bench, linked both hands behind his head and gazed up at the perfectly blue sky. 'So, how *is* the foot?' he asked. 'Mended?'

'Completely,' Santi replied. 'Doctors, physios; they all say what I need now is time out on the pitch.'

'Yeah, but—'

'What?'

'Well, the way you were bigging up Torres and Villa made it sound as though maybe you don't think you'll get to play, or maybe only as a sub.'

'I'm here, Gav,' Santi said with a smile. 'A few weeks ago I didn't think that was possible, but I made it. Like you said, it was hard work, but I had a lot of support too; from the club, from Roz, even from Enrique.'

Gavin nodded. 'And what's the news with him? When we spoke on the phone you said he'd decided to give up at Newcastle.'

'It's just the same. He says he's going home when I get back from here.'

'Yeah, but you know what teenagers are like; always changing their mind.'

'Not Enrique, not this time. At least I don't think so. It's up to him, of course, but I'm worried that somewhere down the line he'll regret throwing away the greatest opportunity he ever had.'

Gavin sat up and turned to face Santi. 'You don't have time to worry about Enrique. Not right now. All you have to worry about for the next few weeks is making it into the team. *You* might never get another chance.'

'I know that, Gav,' said Santi. 'And I'll do my best to make the team. I often think about the advice you gave me last Christmas when we spoke about the World Cup. D'you remember it?'

Gavin looked puzzled and then shook his head. 'I'm always giving advice; it's not always good.'

'Oh, it was good,' said Santi. 'You said all I could do was keep on keeping on. And that's exactly what I'm doing.'

Thirty-one

The spectacular opening ceremony was over, the greatest footballers on the planet were gathered together to celebrate the greatest game on the planet.

Throughout the country, in nine cities covering the length and breadth of the nation, from Cape Town and Port Elizabeth in South, up to Durban, Bloemfontain, Johannesburg and Pretoria, Rustenburg and Nelspruit, and finally to Polokwane in the north, football was on everyone's lips and in everyone's mind.

The official 2010 World Cup Mascot, a goldcoloured, dreadlock-sporting, football-carrying, cuddly leopard in a South African T-shirt who went by the name of Zakumi was in evidence everywhere – on billboards, buses, in shop windows and in the arms of souvenir hunters.

The opening match, in which the host nation had battled to a creditable draw against France, had been played out in front of more than ninety-four thousand fans at the hugely impressive and totally refurbished Soccer City Stadium in Johannesburg, where the final would also take place in a month's time.

Now the tournament was well and truly underway. Football fans from all over the globe had poured into the South African cities in their hundreds of thousands in a riot of colour and, in the main, good humour.

Sombrero-wearing Mexicans paraded in the streets alongside Viking-helmeted Swedes, Brazilians danced sambas in the grandstands, Nigerians in full national dress joked with brave, bare-chested Australians. Every continent was represented; every team was accompanied by flag-waving, face-painted legions of adoring fans.

Spare tickets for the top matches were as rare as gold dust, and fans without tickets could watch the matches at specially created fan zones or gather in open-air bars to sit and relax while watching the games on massive plasma screen televisions.

The first group games were throwing up interesting fixtures and the odd surprise result. Every team wanted to get off to great start, a defeat in the very first match made qualification for the knock-out stages not impossible but much more difficult.

But for Santiago Muñez, the first group match proved to be a disappointing experience. He didn't make the team, and even more frustratingly, he didn't even make the bench.

It was a difficult opener against Paraguay, one of the leading teams from the incredibly tough South American qualifying group. Ten South American nations, all of them bristling with quality and World Cup history, had battled it out for two years and eighteen rounds of qualification matches for only four guaranteed places at the finals.

Paraguay were strong in all departments, particularly upfront where Roque Santa Cruz and Nelson Valdez led the line with strength, skill and, in qualification, a hatful of goals. The Paraguayan team had surprised many, but not themselves, with a two–nil victory over Brazil in the qualifiers, and they certainly had not travelled to South Africa just to make up the numbers.

The team had come a long way since its one–nil defeat by England in the opening group match at the last World Cup and this time the whole squad was determined that the campaign would not end in defeat, even though they were facing the current European champions.

The match started cautiously, as so often happens in opening championship encounters where no one wants to give away a potentially crucial goal. With so much attacking talent on both sides it was strange, but almost predictable, that goals were hard to come by.

The first half ended scoreless, and throughout the forty-five minutes, Santi, sitting with the other squad members behind the selected substitutes, could only watch in frustration, knowing that he could contribute nothing to the cause that day.

Both managers made changes midway through the second period, but as the match wore on without a goal, both teams became more and more cautious and less prepared to make speculative attacking forays.

It wasn't turning out to be the goal feast that some had predicted and many had hoped for and it looked as though it would end in the least popular score for any neutral watchers – nil–nil.

But then, with only six minutes left on the clock, Paraguay scored in a sudden breakaway move. Casillas could only parry a stinging shot from Santa Cruz and as the ball bounced free, midfielder Christian Riveros, following up, skilfully guided the ball home through a mass of legs and bodies.

Spain were stunned – this wasn't the way the campaign was meant to begin. As the Paraguayan defenders shut up shop, a composed Spanish defence switched instantly to all-out attack, which brought the extra threat of a breakaway goal from their opponents.

The Spanish flags in the arena were drooping

sadly as thousands of Spanish fans looked on in despair.

Until a minute before the end.

Cesc Fàbregas, on as a substitute, conjured up a moment of magic, surging down the middle to beat his marker and drive a powerful shot that curved away from the diving keeper and cracked into the net.

Paraguayan defenders thumped the ground in despair while relief was written all over Spanish faces – on the pitch and on the bench, and in the squad seats further back, where Santi was on his feet shouting and applauding as loudly as everyone else.

'Are you OK about it?'

Santi hesitated for a moment before replying, 'Sure I am, darling. The boss can only call it as he sees it. If he'd have wanted me on the pitch or on the bench, I'd have been there.'

'But you might have made the difference.'

'Maybe. I just have to hope I get a chance next time.'

Santi and Roz were speaking on the phone.

They spoke every evening, but that didn't stop either of them from missing the other one.

'How's Rosie?' Santi asked.

'She's fine. Misses you, like I do.'

'Me too, darling.'

Santi had stopped asking Roz if Enrique had changed his mind about leaving England, he knew it was pointless.

'How's your work?' he asked.

He heard Roz sigh. 'Very busy. Sometimes I wish I'd decided to be a WAG after all.'

Santi laughed. 'It wouldn't suit you, darling.'

'Oh, by the way, Gavin was on television summarizing for the England game. He was really good, funny.'

'Yeah, I heard about it. And England did well. Two–nil is a great start.'

'Come on, England!'

'Hey,' said Santi, pretending to be offended. 'You're meant to be on my side.'

'I am,' laughed Roz. 'I'm on both sides.'

'Yeah, but what if we get to play England?'

'Mmm,' said Roz, hesitating for a moment,

'I'm not sure about that. I'll think about it and let you know.'

Santi laughed. 'Well, don't think for too long. We need all the support we can get now.'

'I just want to see you out there for the next match, Santi. We all do. Enrique said you should have been playing today.'

'Hey, that's good. At least he's on my side.'

'We all are, you know that. And don't forget, we're all really proud of you.'

Thirty-two

All over the world, newspaper headlines were screaming out the verdicts on their international teams' first World Cup matches. Some blazed with excitement and optimism, others were more quietly confident and some were filled with gloom and doom.

The back page match reports gave the hard facts on the ninety plus minutes played out in stadiums across South Africa. On the inside back pages, reporters, columnists and former players and managers dissected and analysed the performances of individuals, teams and managers. No mistake was left unmentioned; no tactical bloomer was forgotten or forgiven.

England's two–nil victory received guarded praise. The English press had been scathing of the national team's failure to even reach the 2008 European Championships with the so-called 'golden generation' players. Some of those players still made up the spine of the team; this was surely their last opportunity of glory at a major international tournament. The press as well as the millions of English football fans desperately yearned for success. But so did the press and fans of thirty-one other nations.

The Spanish press remained calm, despite what could be seen as a disappointing first result. At other tournaments, the Spanish had often flattered to deceive, storming away with fantastic early results and then falling short when the going got tougher.

So there was no clamour for wholesale changes to the team; perhaps a less barnstorming start was for the good, and Spain were not the only footballing big guns to slightly misfire in their opening match. But even so, the press reminded the Spanish players and management that the next match had to end in victory, nothing else would do.

The squad and the coaches were perfectly aware of that fact. One draw was not critical at this stage, but another might be, and a second match defeat would almost certainly be fatal. So, although there was no hint of panic when the videotapes of the Paraguay match were studied, everyone was aware that in the next match, the individual and team performances had to go up by a good few notches.

One positive of the Paraguay match for the Spanish squad was that there had been no significant injuries: apart from a few minor bruises all the players had come through unscathed.

When training resumed it appeared as though the starting eleven for the second match would be the same as for the first. Santi worked increasingly hard as he grew more and more certain that his metatarsal was back to full strength, but in the practice games he remained in the second-string line-up – the preferred striking partnership was still Torres and Villa.

But Santi knew he was looking and feeling especially sharp. And he was trying to stay focused and positive, telling himself that the metatarsal break, which had so disrupted his season, at least meant that he wasn't exhausted after a long Premiership campaign. He felt as fresh as he would at the start of a season.

And his patience and persistence in training paid off, not completely and not with a place in the starting line-up for the second group match against Australia. But he was on the bench. It was a start; Santi's World Cup was about to begin.

Australia is another of those national teams made up almost entirely of players who play their club football away from their home country. The Socceroos, as they are affectionately known, had been making big impacts at club level across the globe for many years.

Players like Mark Viduka, Tim Cahill, Harry Kewell, Mark Schwarzer and Lucas Neill had been fixtures in the Premiership and other top leagues for season after season.

And although some of the top names had quit the international scene and others were reaching the veteran stage, the Socceroos were still a force to be reckoned with.

They'd come through the demanding forty-three nation strong Asian Football Confederation qualification competition, having switched from the Oceania Football Confederation back in 2006.

It had been a long journey, one that the Aussies wanted to continue for as long as possible. They were a hard team, and a good one; it wasn't going to be an easy second match for the Spanish.

Back in the 2006 finals, the Socceroos had progressed smoothly through the group stages, going out in the last sixteen to eventual world champions, Italy. And before the match with Spain, some of their battle-hardened players were telling the press that they intended going at least that far again.

Santi stood in pouring rain with the other substitutes as the anthems played and players and supporters sang proudly. He couldn't believe how quickly the weather had changed from last week's bright sun.

The atmosphere was fantastic; soccer fans were travelling huge distances by bus and train just to reach the stadiums. And once they arrived they were determined to enjoy themselves, particularly the Aussies; a little inconvenience like bitterly cold, heavy rain wasn't going to stop many of them from going bare-chested.

The floodlights were cutting through the driving rain, and up in the television galleries Gavin Harris was sitting next to the match commentator, preparing to add his observations and expert opinion.

Gavin knew most of the players on the pitch – many were personal friends – but his best mate was warming the Spanish bench. Gavin was hoping for an exciting match, but most of all he was hoping that his friend Santi would get on for his first taste of World Cup action.

It came a lot sooner than Gavin or even Santi would have expected. The heavy rain was making the playing surface treacherous and the newly laid turf was cutting up in places.

It was one of those unfortunate situations. Given better weather and little more time to bed in, the pitch would probably have been perfect. But the downpour, which had come hot on the heels of another one the previous day, was turning the match into something of a lottery.

Just after the twenty minutes mark, the Spanish attacking midfielder, David Silva, skidded and went down after a chase for the ball. He got up rubbing his right calf and soon after signalled to the bench that the leg was giving him some trouble. This early in the tournament there was no point in taking unnecessary risks, so the manager signalled that he should come off.

Santi had been warming up with the other Spanish subs, but he was surprised to see his number come up on the board to indicate that he was going on.

'And it's Santiago Muñez going on for David Silva,' said Gavin from his commentary position. 'Bit of a shock, that, a striker replacing a midfielder. Spain are obviously looking for goals.'

The surprise substitution was probably fortunate for Santi; he didn't have time to get nervous about it. One minute he was jogging on the touchline, the next his tracksuit was off and he was on the pitch.

He slotted into a position just behind the front two, and for a few minutes struggled to get used to the pace of the game, particularly as the ground was heavy and draining.

The downpour showed no signs of giving up and was making skilful play with the ball on the ground almost impossible. Both teams were reverting to long or high balls and struggling to string passes together to mount meaningful attacks. The first half ended with frustration written on all the faces of both sets of players.

Up in the commentary box, as Gavin discussed the few highlights from the first period, he made it clear that the poor standard of play seen so far was not down to the players.

Raindrops pounded against the window and ran down the glass as Gavin watched a replay of a Spanish attack. 'Everyone's doing their best,' he said to camera, 'but this rain's making the sort of football we hoped for impossible. I feel sorry for the players; this is a game that could be decided by a mistake. No one wants to see that, not at the World Cup.' He looked away from the television monitor to the rain-streaked window. 'It's just like home. Reminds me of Newcastle on a wet Friday night.'

Maybe it reminded Santi of Newcastle too, because despite the downpour he was enjoying every minute of the match and looked to be one of the few players comparatively comfortable in the conditions.

Midway through the second period, he ran onto a drilled cross and hit a shot from thirty yards that beat the keeper and thundered against the crossbar.

Santi turned away, shouting in frustration, and up in the commentary box Gavin laughed.

'He meant that,' he told watching millions. 'Muñez is playing well.'

He was, but the game was still goalless.

With fifteen minutes left, Fernando Torrez found himself in possession out wide on the right.

David Villa was in the centre looking for the cross, which Torres hit high and hard, a little too hard for Villa who jumped for the ball but had no chance of reaching it.

But Santi did. He came ghosting in at the back post and met the cross perfectly with his head sending it past the keeper and into the net.

'Terrific goal!' shouted Gavin up in the commentary box. 'Santiago Muñez, back for Spain, back to his best, back of the net!'

Thirty-three

It wasn't the most stunning or satisfying of wins, but it was a win and that was what mattered most at this stage of the campaign.

The immediate post-match inquest and the press interviews were over, and Santi was back at the hotel. He had telephone calls to make, and he'd promised that tonight the first would be to his most honest critic and, as far as Santi was concerned, the most knowledgeable football expert of all – his grandmother, Mercedes.

Santi knew, before she even picked up the phone, that Mercedes would have watched every second of the match in her home in Los Angeles, and that many of her neighbours would also have been squeezed around the television, enjoying the game and listening to Mercedes' running commentary.

She answered the telephone after just three rings. 'Is that you, Santiago?'

'Hi, Grandma, how are you?'

'That first shot, the one that hit the bar, you should have kept it down.' Mercedes didn't waste her words when she had something on her mind.

Santi grinned. 'Yes, Grandma.'

'You got over the ball. I told you about that so many times before.'

'Yes, Grandma.'

'And you could have set up another goal, late on. But you held onto the ball for too long, you were greedy.'

'Yes, Grandma.'

'I don't know how you expect Spain to win the thing if you don't all step up the work rate. Look at Sven Goran Eriksson, with the Mexican side; he's got them working as a unit. Very good, very very good. And England, another win, they look dangerous.'

'You're right, Grandma.'

'I'm always right.'

Santi smiled and shook his head. There was no arguing with that. Mercedes was always right, or almost always, and it wasn't worth arguing about the times she wasn't.

'Oh, yes,' she continued, almost as an afterthought. 'The goal you scored, very good, you took it well.'

Santi almost collapsed back onto the bed; praise from his grandmother was praise indeed.

They spoke for a little longer, with Mercedes giving her grandson the benefit of her football expertise before asking about her great-granddaughter, Rosie, and then Santi chatted briefly to his other brother, Julio.

Julio was no great football fan, but he was fiercely proud of his brother, Santi, and of his achievements and never missed a televised match when Santi was playing.

As they spoke, the conversation was interrupted time and again by Julio having to say, *Oh, and Grandma says this*, or *Grandma says that* before passing on another pearl of footballing wisdom from Mercedes.

They ended the call with promises to meet up after the tournament was over and then Santi called Roz. She was ecstatic about Santi's goal-scoring appearance from the bench, and unlike Mercedes had not a single word of criticism.

'You were brilliant. Gavin said on television that you were back to your best.'

'Really?' said a delighted Santi. 'I don't know about that, but it felt good out there today.'

'Oh, and he also said that a Muñez headed goal was a collector's item and that you should stick the photos of it in your scrapbook.'

Santi laughed. 'I don't remember Gavin being the greatest header of the ball either.'

They spoke for a long time – about Rosie, about Santi's call to his grandmother, and about how they missed each other. Even though Santi was enjoying every minute of the tournament, he still felt homesick and missed his family.

'And what about Enrique?' he said at last, moving on to the subject they both knew they needed to discuss the most. 'How is he?'

Roz hesitated before replying, 'He watched

the match and said you played well, and you know how critical he is, even of you.'

'Almost as bad as my grandmother.'

'But he's not very talkative right now.'

'You don't think he's getting into more trouble?' Santi was immediately concerned.

'No, I'm certain he isn't. It's not like before.'

'So what is it?'

'It's his decision to leave,' said Roz. 'I'm sure it's still playing on his mind.'

Thirty-four

It was only a matter of time before a team received the full Spanish treatment, when everything and everyone finally clicked into place, with defence, midfield and attack functioning as a complete unit.

That team was Cameroon.

Santi made the starting eleven for the final group match and was part of a Spanish masterclass in pass and move.

The Indomitable Lions, as Cameroon are known, are a proud and brave footballing outfit, having qualified for more World Cup finals than any other African nation, and in Samuel Eto'o they have a truly world-class striker. But this was the match where it all came right for Spain.

The hours spent on the training ground; the one-touch precision, the set piece moves, the overlaps, the dummy runs, everything worked perfectly and soon the cries of, 'Ole, ole, ole, ole,' were echoing around the stadium.

Santi scored one before going off to avoid too much pressure on his foot, and there were further goals from David Villa and Fernando Torres, who grabbed two.

Suddenly, Spain were back up there as favourites, but other nations – mainly the usual suspects like Italy, West Germany, Brazil, Argentina and even England – were looking very strong as the tournament moved into the second phase. There were just sixteen nations left to battle for the trophy now, including host nation South Africa, who had put in a storming series of games to finish as runners-up in their group.

The completion of the group games had shown the qualifiers their potential route to the final, revealing that Spain would face England in the semifinal should both teams reach that far. It was an intriguing and tantalizing prospect but no one, players or management in either camp, dared to think that far ahead for more than a few moments. There was a long way to go before a semifinal could be contemplated.

As group winners, Spain were facing one of the runners-up from another group. It sounded good on paper, but those runners-up just happened to be Holland, who in a tight group had slipped to a surprise and unlucky defeat – to an increasingly impressive USA team – before winning their following two matches.

The Dutch were a formidable outfit, powerful in all departments, especially up front where, despite the international retirement of Ruud van Nistelrooy, there were still forwards of the quality of Robin van Persie, Arjen Robben and Dirk Kuyt.

And Holland had come through a tough group for the second successive major tournament. At Euro 2008 they had topped the so-called 'Group of Death' with maximum points, beating Italy, France and Romania. They had gone into the next round in outstanding form and been hotly tipped to win the tournament but, to most people's surprise, they had been beaten 3–1 by Russia.

Now they were set to face Spain in the World Cup second round, and fans of both teams in South Africa, and television viewers around the globe, looked forward to a match between two of Europe's heavyweights.

And the encounter didn't disappoint, starting as a slow burner but gradually hotting up to become a World Cup classic, a match that was destined to be discussed, remembered and replayed on television screens for many years to come.

Early on though, it looked as though two stylish teams, one pass and move, the other the latest brand of Dutch Total Football, would nullify the other's threat.

Santi was back on the bench – not because of the metatarsal, but because he'd noticed a slight tightening of his hamstrings after the previous match. The physio told him it was only to be expected; his body had had a long lay-off and was still getting used to the stresses and strains of full-time training and playing.

That was no real consolation for Santi as he sat with the other subs watching the opening exchanges of the last sixteen encounter. It was cautious to begin with, both teams fully aware that there were no second chances now. One mistake might very well be the last mistake.

The game was pacy but cagy, tactical and technical. For a long time it was almost like an exhibition match, a demonstration of how the beautiful game could and should be played.

It wasn't lacking in passion, and there were darting runs, committed tackles, shots that demanded saves from keepers Casillas and van de Sar, but for a long period there was the feeling that a volcano was bubbling but not erupting.

But then it did, deep into the second half. Santi was on by now, and the spectre of extra time and possible penalties to follow looked as though it might become reality.

The match had been hard but fair, one player on either side picking up a yellow card for over-zealous challenges, both of whom had subsequently been substituted to avoid the threat of a red and a ban for the next match.

Suddenly Dirk Kuyt, operating wide out right as he did so often in the red shirt of Liverpool, cut inside and bore down on the goal. Sergio Ramos, a rock in the Spanish defence, closed in and made the tackle, which the referee judged to be unfair, sounding the whistle for a Dutch free kick.

It was in perfect shooting range, and as the Spanish wall formed, Kuyt, van Persie and Robben hovered around the ball, all looking poised to strike.

When the whistle sounded again, Robben made the feint, Kuyt the dummy run and van Persie the strike, expertly bending it around the wall and past the despairing dive of Casillas. The Dutch players and fans went mad and the orange flags billowed around one half of the stadium.

But the goal spurred Spain into renewed effort and their football turned from brilliant to dazzling. One move racked up no fewer than fourteen passes from defence through midfield, finishing with a Villa shot which thundered against an upright. And while the crowd was still buzzing from that, Spain grabbed an equalizer, midfielder Fàbregas finishing close in from a Muñez pass.

It was all to play for, but before either team could snatch a winner the whistle sounded for the end of ninety minutes. They were going to extra time.

The next half hour would be thirty minutes – thirty-two with stoppage time – that would enter World Cup folklore.

It was non-stop, totally committed and totally absorbing play, which no one in the stadium would ever forget.

Spain took the lead with only two minutes of extra time played, Torres steering in a dropping ball headed on from the edge of the box.

But rather than sit back and shut up shop, looking to see out the remainder of the match, they went all out in search of a third. And for every attack the Spanish made, the Dutch came back at them with an attack of their own. Keepers made brilliant saves, defenders made last-gasp tackles, the woodwork at both ends took a pounding, but as the teams changed over for the final period, the score remained the same and penalties loomed even closer.

But the momentum shifted yet again with ten minutes remaining when Dutch midfielder Wesley Sneijder came from deep to net the equalizer with a bullet header.

Both teams could have been forgiven then for going on the defensive and opting for the lottery of penalties. Neither team did; the all-out barrage on goal continued at both ends.

With less than a minute of stoppage time remaining on the clock, Edwin van de Sar rose to punch out a dangerous cross. The ball spun high towards Santi, who was on the edge of the box. Defenders closed in; there was no time to allow the ball to bounce. Santi struck the volley perfectly, and from the moment boot made contact with ball there was no doubt where the latter would finish up – in the net.

Holland were stunned, Spain were ecstatic, and even though the match restarted there was no time to mount another attack. The whistle sounded and players on both sides sank to their knees, anguish written all over the faces of the Dutch and joy on the faces of the Spanish.

Applause and cheers rang down from every corner of the stadium; even the Dutch supporters were on their feet, cheering not only the gallant losers but also the Spanish for their part in the magnificent spectacle of football.

The full magnitude of the knock-out stages of the finals was really hitting home to Santi as he acknowledged the rapturous cheers of the Spanish fans. He'd scored the winner, but at that moment he really did believe that the goal-scorer's cliché of the result mattering more than scoring was absolutely true. Spain were through to the quarterfinals: the dream was still alive, very much alive.

Thirty-five

'Three goals so far, two of them the winning goals, not bad for someone who didn't even think he'd be playing in the tournament.'

Santi nodded. 'It's gone better than I could have imagined, Gav. It's incredible.'

The Spanish players had been given a well-earned day off after their victory over Holland and Santi and Gavin were relaxing together over a drink.

Santi was drinking nothing stronger than mineral water, but Gavin, who'd been known to polish off several bottles of vintage champagne in a single session in his playboy heyday, was allowing himself a single glass of bubbly.

'Here's to you, Santi,' he said, raising the glass in a toast. 'You deserve your day off.'

Santi raised his own glass in acknowledgement. 'How about you, how's your tournament going?'

'I'm certainly clocking up the air miles,' said Gavin. 'It's a big country and I've just about covered most of it to be at matches. Got a few days off now though, before my next match.'

'What you planning to do with them? Some sightseeing?'

Gavin raised both eyebrows and took a sip at his champagne. 'Santi, when did you ever hear me talk about sightseeing? Sightseeing is not on my list of the hundred things I must do before I die. No, mate, I shall be relaxing by the pool.' He raised the champagne glass again. 'Enjoying a few glasses of this and looking forward to the lovely Luisa joining me out here.'

'Hey, that's great,' said Santi. 'I wish Roz was here with me.'

'So why isn't she?'

'Work mainly. And we didn't know if I'd get to

play, or how far we'd make it through the competition.'

'Yeah, but now you're in the quarters; could she get the time off?'

'I guess,' said Santi with a shrug of his shoulders. 'But I don't like to suggest it now, there's such a lot happening at home. She's been brilliant, Gav, 'specially with Enrique. She's been there for him when I couldn't.'

'I always told you Roz was a great girl, didn't I?'

Santi smiled and took a sip of water. 'You know, I still feel like I let Enrique down.'

'Oh, don't be crazy.'

'But I do. I should have seen he was having problems and done something about it. Then maybe we wouldn't have got to the situation we're in now. I just wish I could make it up to him somehow.'

Gavin finished his champagne and for once said nothing. He put down the glass, sat back in his chair and nodded slowly, looking extremely thoughtful.

* * *

Roz could have her fill of football. Quite easily. She always wanted to see Santi play, even though sometimes she got so nervous she couldn't bear to watch. But as for other games, when Santi wasn't involved, she could take it or leave it.

That's why she was out in the garden with Rosie while Enrique sat in the house, glued to the television screen. He wasn't even watching a live match, just endless replays and analysis of the last sixteen matches.

Enrique couldn't get enough of football: he lived and breathed it, just as Santi had told Roz he'd lived and breathed the game when he was his young brother's age. That was partly why Roz was so concerned about Enrique's future when he went back to Spain. If no club with a youth development scheme was prepared to take a chance on him after he'd walked out on Newcastle, then Roz feared he might easily fall into the wrong company and the wrong ways, as he had before.

The garden looked lovely. Light rain the previous evening had refreshed the lawn and brought a new burst of colour to the summer flowers.

Roz was sitting in the early evening sunshine, her head in a book, while Rosie played on the grass nearby. The book was a chick lit novel, the sort of light read Roz enjoyed when she needed to escape from the harsh realities of her job. But this evening she was finding it difficult to concentrate and it wasn't down to work. The problem of Enrique was at the front of her mind.

She heard a noise and looked up to see Enrique walking towards her.

'Don't tell me you've had enough of football?' Roz said with a smile. 'Or has the television broken?'

'There's someone here.'

'Oh, who is it?'

'It's . . . it's . . . I don't know how he can be here. But he is.'

'Who?

'In a car.'

'Yes, I guessed that much, but who's in a car?'

'I heard the car and I saw him through the

window and I came to tell you before he got out and came to the door.'

'Enrique, will you please tell me who it *is*?'

Suddenly a familiar figure appeared from around the side of the house. 'It's me, darling. Who else?'

Roz stared. 'Gavin. I don't believe it. *Gavin!*'

'You must be exhausted.'

Gavin grinned his usual cheeky grin. 'To be honest, I am a bit cream-crackered, but once I'd made up my mind what I was going to do I just got on with it.'

Roz was still reeling from the shock of Gavin's arrival, followed by his announcement that he'd come to take her and Enrique back with him to South Africa to watch Santi in the quarterfinal.

'Of course, if they get through that, then you can stay on for the semis,' he continued. 'And then if they . . . no, I'd better not go on, don't want to tempt fate, do we?'

Enrique had been in awe of Gavin since he'd first met him back in the Madrid days, but when he heard the South African plan he just gawped, unable to say a word.

'So what d'you think?' Gavin said, beaming at Roz. 'Great idea, eh? But we need to move quickly, so you'd both better start packing.'

Enrique went to sprint up the stairs to throw a few things into a bag, but Roz was quick to stop him. 'Hang on, hang on,' she said. She turned to Gavin. 'Look, it's a lovely idea, Gavin, but it's impossible, for me at least.'

'Why's that then?' said Gavin.

'There's . . . there's so much I have to do here. There's Rosie, work, this place, I can't just drop everything and go.' She saw the crestfallen look on Enrique's face. 'Maybe you could take Enrique,' she said. 'But as for me, Gav, I'd really love to go, but there's no way I can.'

Gavin just smiled. 'There's always a way, Roz, trust me.'

Thirty-six

The plane was cruising at thirty-eight thousand feet, midway into the twelve-hour flight. Roz was dozing, Gavin was making notes about the World Cup quarterfinals he would be commenting on, and Enrique had just finished watching a film, too excited to even think about sleeping.

He stared out through the window into the night sky. Thousands of stars were glittering, lighting up the inky darkness. It was all so amazing, almost unbelievable, but they truly were on their way to South Africa.

Gavin had been confident that everything could be sorted, and it had been. Roz's mum, Carol, was only too delighted to take charge of

Rosie for a few days, and Rosie was delighted to go to her granny, especially when she was allowed to pack her own case for her 'holiday'.

Lorraine would still be looking after Rosie during the day and Jamie was happy to keep an eye on the house – in return, he told Gavin, for an England shirt signed by Wayne Rooney. Gavin, of course, said it would be no problem.

Roz was due some holiday, and with a little help from her friends at the hospital she was able to swap the shifts she was already committed to. Her workmates turned out to be as keen as Gavin for her to see Santi play in the World Cup.

Everything was organized, and when Gavin phoned Santi to tell him what he'd arranged, Santi was over the moon.

Which was exactly how Enrique was feeling as he stared from the window and saw the huge creamy ball of the moon hanging in the night sky. He felt a tap on his arm and turned.

Gavin was slipping the notes he'd made into a folder. 'Just been thinking about the quarterfinal matches,' he said. 'Some terrific teams, who d'you fancy to go through?'

For the next five minutes, Enrique gave his considered opinion and his predictions, based on what Gavin quickly recognized was an awesome knowledge of the game. He sat and listened, nodding occasionally, throwing in a question or a comment when one was required, but mainly just enjoying what Enrique had to say.

When he finally fell silent, Gavin nodded again and then said, 'So, you still like football then?'

Enrique looked confused. 'Like it? I love football. I always have loved football, I always will love football.'

'Mmm,' said Gavin, with a look that said he didn't quite believe what Enrique was saying. 'So why is it you're giving it up?'

Enrique blushed with embarrassment and for a moment said nothing. 'I'm not giving it up, just giving it up in Newcastle, and in England.'

'Oh, I see. So you don't like Newcastle?'

'No, I like it very much, apart from the weather. And I've made some good friends at the academy and at school too now.'

'England then, you don't like England?'

'No, I do like England. It's a good place to be. And to live.'

Gavin nodded. 'Right, so you do like football, you do like Newcastle, you do like England, but you're giving up football in Newcastle, England?'

Enrique sighed. 'I know. I know it sounds crazy. And in many ways I don't want to go.'

'Have you told Santi and Roz that?'

'No,' said Enrique with a shake of his head. 'Because they are the main reason I'm going. And it's not because I don't like being with them, because I do, very much.'

Gavin grinned. 'Somehow I knew you'd say that.'

'The reason I have to go is because I let Santi and Roz down so badly. I know they would give me another chance, they already have, but I don't feel like I deserve any more chances. Not here, anyway. I have to go home and start again.'

'You mean, you want to make it as difficult as you can for yourself to become a pro footballer? Give yourself the punishment you think you deserve?'

Enrique thought for a moment and then nodded. 'Yes, I guess that is it.'

An air steward wandered down the aisle offering tea or coffee and Gavin asked for some coffee.

He took a sip as the steward moved on and then turned to Enrique again. 'You know, we've all messed up in our time, one way or another. I came close to ruining my career more than once and Santi almost walked out on Newcastle soon after he arrived, when things weren't going right. Did you know that?'

'No, I didn't.'

'No, you've only known him since he was a big star at Real Madrid. But he had it tough too, really tough. And the thing I admire most about Santi, although I'd never tell him this 'cos he'd get too bigheaded, is that he never gave up. He could have done, so many times, but he had a dream and he wouldn't let it go.' Enrique didn't reply, but Gavin could see he was deep in thought as he continued. 'From what I hear, you've got a pretty special talent. To my mind, you'd be best to take this fantastic opportunity you've got at

Newcastle, knowing that Santi and Roz are completely behind you. You messed up, but it's over now and it's time to move on, not run away.' He paused for a moment and then shrugged. 'But what do I know? I'm just a television pundit now.'

'And quite a good manager,' Enrique said.

Gavin laughed. 'We'll see about that.' He checked his watch. 'You ought to try to get some sleep, you've got a pretty full day to come.'

Enrique smiled and then sank down in his seat and closed his eyes.

Gavin looked over at Roz on the far side of Enrique. Her eyes were open and Gavin winked at her.

'Thank you,' she mouthed silently.

Thirty-seven

The quarterfinals in the lower half of the draw had tantalizingly paired Spain against Argentina and England against Mexico, the side now managed by the former England boss, Sven Goran Eriksson. It was another of those wonderful coincidences that football so often throws up.

The top half featured surprise package Nigeria, along with Germany, France and Brazil. Many of the heavyweight footballing nations had risen to the top of the pile now that the tournament was coming to the business end, although holders Italy were missing, having gone out in a match decided by penalties. And South Africa, too, had come to the end of their run – though not without a hard-fought second-round match that went to extra time.

With only eight teams now remaining, every squad and every player was totally focused on the next match, knowing there was everything to play for and that a place in the World Cup final, and football history, was only two matches away.

Santi was overjoyed that Roz and Enrique had arrived to watch the meeting with Argentina, although he wouldn't get to see them until after the match, which was being played at the Coca Cola Park Stadium in Johannesburg. The Spanish squad had arrived in the city a few days earlier but Roz and Enrique flew in just hours before the kick-off.

The stadium, formerly known as the Ellis Park Stadium, had hosted the Rugby World Cup final back in 1995. It had undergone a major refurbishment in the run up to the current tournament and could now seat 65,000 spectators. And every seat would be filled, as the match was a sell-out. As always, a few seats had been left vacant for last minute VIP guests, and Gavin had managed to pull a few strings and bag one each for Roz and Enrique.

Gavin himself would be up in one of the TV commentary boxes, summarizing and assessing the semifinal opponents for England. If, of course, England beat Mexico. As soon as this match was over, Gavin was flying off to the southern coastal city of Port Elizabeth, where England and Mexico were meeting the following day for their quarterfinal match at the Nelson Mandela Bay Stadium.

But Santi and his team-mates were doing their utmost, like every other player still in the tournament, to stick to the old football adage – take one match at a time. Thinking too much of what might lie ahead could turn out to be fatal.

Argentina were formidable opponents, being twice former World Cup winners. And even though the last of those victories was back in 1986, the current Argentina side was bristling with world-class players, including Lionel Messi, Carlos Tévez and Javier Mascherano.

Messi and Mascherano had been part of the Argentina team which had successfully defended its Olympic football title in Beijing in 2008, and Tévez was the leading goal-scorer at the previous Olympics in Athens 2004. Mascherano had also played in that tournament and consequently become the first Argentine ever to win two Olympic gold medals.

Those three players formed the nucleus of the Argentina squad, which was strong in every department.

Neutral observers sometimes suggested that, despite having the fantastic talents of Messi, Tévez and the relative newcomer Sergio Agüero up front, without the presence of Hernán Crespo who had averaged better than a goal every two international games Argentina suffered from the lack of a proven and prolific out and out goal-scorer.

But the new wave had been scoring from all positions during the tournament, with defenders and particularly midfielders providing goals as well as assists. The threat to the Spanish goal could come from almost any area of the pitch, but particularly from wherever the genius Lionel Messi happened to be.

It promised to be a fascinating encounter.

The two sets of players sang their national anthems, some more confidently and tunefully than others, as the television camera panned along the line-ups.

Voices all around the stadium rang out, and the red and yellow flags of Spain waved on one side and the blue and white of Argentina on the other.

As the second anthem came to an end and the two teams shook hands, the excitement rose even further. And as the players trotted away to take up their positions for the kick-off the applause and cheers thundered around the stadium.

Santi knew approximately where Roz and Enrique were sitting. He waved, not certain that he could see them but certain that they would be looking at him.

And then the whistle sounded and the match was underway.

'What a goal! What an incredible strike!'

Gavin Harris sat back in his television

commentary box seat and shook his head in disbelief. The deadlock was finally broken, just five minutes before the end of the first half.

The teams had been evenly matched and chances had been hard to come by. But then, thirty-five yards out from the Spanish goal, Carlos Tévez went down in a tussle for the ball. It looked, to most, a hard but fair challenge, the sort of tackle that nine times out of ten would have been shrugged away by most referees. But not this one and not this time. He blew for the foul and quickly waved away the protests of the Spanish players.

Lionel Messi placed the ball carefully. It was just about level with the left-hand edge of the penalty box as he looked at it. A couple more Argentine players lingered close by, but it was obvious to everyone that Messi was going to take the free kick.

He waited for the whistle, eyes weighing up the target as the ref paced out ten yards for the Spanish defenders and Iker Casillas shouted frantic instructions to the five-man wall. They shuffled one way and then edged back a little, until he signalled that he was satisfied with their positioning.

The stadium fell almost silent and the piercing sound of the whistle echoed around the rafters.

Tévez made the dummy run and then Messi glided forward. The position of the ball offered him a near or far post option for his attempt, the near post being easier.

But great players rarely take the easy option. The ball flew out wide and curved around the far side of the wall, spinning viciously all the time. It cut back at an almost impossible angel and arced into the far, top corner of the net, giving Casillas absolutely no chance.

It was an amazing strike, difficult to believe, but there was no mistaking that the ball was nestling in the back of the net and that Messi was racing away in triumph as the Argentinian flags waved and the supporters shouted and yelled their worship.

The Spaniards looked stunned. Conceding the opening goal minutes before the break was a huge psychological blow.

It was vital that Spain didn't lose another goal

before the half ended and Argentina were equally determined to leave the field with their lead intact, so the remaining few minutes before the break were played out cautiously by both teams.

And when the half-time whistle sounded with the score the same, the Argentine players went off looking delighted while the Spanish departed with their heads bowed.

The crowd was still buzzing with excitement and debate over the goal. Up in their seats Enrique was explaining to Roz why the free kick should never have been given, while in the television galleries commentators and pundits were already watching the replays and arguing over whether or not a foul had been committed.

To some it had been a fairly innocuous challenge, to others it was probably a foul and they could see why a free kick had been given. The unarguable fact was that Argentina were leading one–nil.

There were no changes to either side when the match resumed and the Spanish immediately went on the offensive.

Argentina, at first, seemed content to curb

their attacking tendencies by keeping the ball when in possession rather than launching meaningful attacks of their own.

It meant a frustrating opening fifteen minutes to the second half for the Spanish team, which wasn't quite functioning as it had in the previous two matches. Santi was finding it as difficult as the rest of his team-mates as their attacks were broken down time and again.

Spain were living dangerously, with three players up all the time, but they had little choice as the clock ticked down.

They needed a break, a moment of magic, or a moment of good fortune. They got a portion of all three of those.

Santi picked up the ball just over the halfway line. He set off on a surging run, seeing immediately that he was the most forward attacker. His team-mates had been forced to drop deeper as the Argentine defenders pushed up, squeezing the space.

There was no pass on; Santi had to take the ball out wide, while Torres, Villa and the attacking midfielders raced for position.

Using his speed, Santi effortlessly shrugged off a challenge and outpaced his opponent as he neared the edge of the box. The Spanish supporters roared their approval.

Santi should have looked for the pass, there were options opening now. But there was another possibility, a glimpse of goal with the near side almost asking for the shot. Santi didn't need a second invitation, he let fly from thirty yards with a right-foot thunderbolt.

But he hadn't seen the defender closing in as he hit the shot. The ball struck the defender on the shoulder and took a wicked deflection. The keeper was already committed to the dive towards the near post and, in fairness to him, would almost certainly have made the save or at least pushed it behind for a corner. But the ball flew straight across him and straight into the goal just inside the far post.

Spain had got their break, and their equalizer, through a moment of Muñez magic followed by a huge slice of good fortune.

The goal changed the complexion of the match and forced Argentina to go back on to the offensive, which suited them far more than the holding game they had been playing.

But now Spain had the momentum. Their midfield maestros Xavi, Fàbregas and Iniesta began weaving *their* magic, causing panic in the Argentina defence and finally carving out real chances for the strikers.

Santi went close again, Torres had a brilliant diving header saved and then David Villa snatched the winner close in with ten minutes remaining, latching on to a pass from Torres in a move that also involved Santi and the three midfielders.

It was a worthy winner – not the strike itself, which was clinically dispatched by Villa, but the build-up, which had class written all over it.

Even more importantly it had earned Spain its first World Cup semifinal appearance for a full sixty years.

Thirty-eight

The reunion was difficult and slightly awkward for them all, but especially for Roz and Santi. They had been apart for weeks, and although they had spoken almost every day on the phone, coming face-to-face so far from home in unfamiliar surroundings after such a long separation was a little unreal and bizarre.

They were back at the hotel with neither quite sure of what to say, or whether they should be celebrating or catching up. So they ended up doing a bit of both, Roz for once talking about the match in detail and telling Santi how proud she was of him, while he asked questions about Rosie and life back in England.

But Santi was so pleased to see Roz, and Enrique too. Santi was physically and mentally drained after the exhausting match and it was hard to come down from the heights of emotion that had been reached by everyone out on the pitch. But suddenly being with his wife and young brother again was helping him come back down to earth, to detach the drama of the football pitch from the other part of his life. It made him feel better, it was reassuring, and in its special own way it was even more important and exciting.

Roz told him for the third time that she was so, so proud of the way he had played, and that when he scored she couldn't stop herself from crying.

'I don't think I did score,' said Santi smiling. 'I think it's going down as an own goal.'

'But you have to claim it,' said Enrique quickly. 'It was your goal. You went for goal.'

'But the ball didn't go where I meant it to,' laughed Santi. 'Lucky it went in, the guys would have had something to say if it had missed.'

'It would have beaten the keeper anyway, and

you changed the match,' continued Enrique. 'If it wasn't for you, I don't think Spain would have won.'

Santi and Roz exchanged a look; they weren't accustomed to such fulsome praise from Enrique.

Enrique had said very little up until then; he'd mainly stared at his Santi with a newfound look of hero worship, seeming to recognize at last exactly what his brother had gone through and achieved to make it to the World Cup and to play so well.

'I'm glad you're both here,' said Santi. 'And that you can stay on for the semifinal.' He looked at Roz. 'You can stay on, can't you?'

Roz laughed. 'Gavin seems to have organized everything.'

'Yeah, where is he? I haven't thanked him properly for doing this.'

'You'll have to wait for a while,' said Roz. 'He's on a plane to Port Elizabeth.'

'But we *are* staying,' added Enrique quickly. 'We're here for as long as you are. And then . . .' He hesitated and looked a little embarrassed, uncertain how to go on.

'What?' said Santi. 'And then what?'

'I'm . . . I'm going to come back to England; I've decided to stay. I'm going to take the place at the academy.'

He fell silent. No one said a word; Santi and Roz just stared.

'If . . . if that's OK?'

Santi laughed loudly. 'OK? Of course it's OK. It's more than OK. It's fantastic! Eh, Roz?'

Roz smiled and nodded. 'I'm really pleased,' she said to Enrique. 'And you know Rosie will be too.'

'And Gavin,' added Santi. 'I've been talking to Gavin about it. He'll want to know.'

'I shouldn't worry too much about that,' said Roz. She glanced towards Enrique. 'I've a feeling Gavin already knows.'

Sven Goran Eriksson had moulded an impressive Mexican team, skilfully blending youth and experience since taking the reins just before the World Cup qualification rounds began.

His appointment as Mexican manager came as something of a shock back in August of 2008, and he admitted he had never even been to the country before taking the job. But once in position he threw himself enthusiastically into the job and the subsequent qualification results won over the doubters.

Now, in getting Mexico to the quarterfinals of the tournament, he had equalled the nation's best World Cup performances. Mexico made the last eight in both 1970 and 1986, but on both occasions the tournament was on home turf so this was, arguably, their best ever World Cup showing.

Sven was fortunate in having so many of his squad who were used to playing in the tough European leagues; players like Rafael Márquez, Aarón Galindo and the young strikers, Carlos Vela and Giovani dos Santos.

And in the last eight match, Mexico almost pulled off a major shock by knocking out England.

The game was a tight, tactical battle; a goalless first half was followed by dos Santos netting just three minutes into the second period. But the 'goal' was disallowed for being offside. It was a correct if marginal decision but one that seemed to inspire Mexico to even greater efforts.

Sven, on the Mexican bench, must have watched with mixed emotions as his team battled bravely for the win. He had brought many of the English players into the national team during his stewardship of England and he knew most them as well as he knew his current charges.

With twenty minutes remaining, Vela struck an upright from a free kick, but from the resulting loose ball, England scored in a breakaway, Rooney providing Walcott with the pass, which he slotted into one corner.

It was the only goal of the match, and at the final whistle most of the England players made a point of going to Goran Eriksson and shaking his hand before leaving the field.

England were in the semifinals for the first time since 1990. They would meet Spain. It promised to be an epic encounter.

And so did the other semifinal, where five-times winners Brazil were to do battle with three-times winners Germany for the right to a place in yet another World Cup final. It would be a true 'Clash of the Titans', a match worthy of the final itself. The Brazilians were probably just favourites; their journey so far had included many moments of typical swaggering brilliance. But the Germans too had provided moments of genius, coupled with their traditional steel and determination. In truth, and like the other semi-final, it could be anyone's game.

Thirty-nine

The semifinals of the World Cup: everything to play for and everything to lose.

For the two winning teams, there awaits a place in the ultimate match of any professional footballer's career. For the two losers, there awaits a place in a match that is an honour in itself, but a match that few players would choose to play in – the third place play-off.

The Spain versus England match was being played at the new 70,000 plus seat stadium in Durban. It meant another change of location for both teams, but by now they were used to the travel and to the change of base camps.

England were riding high, buoyed up on a

wave of expectation back in the UK. This, at last, appeared to be the tournament in which the so-called 'golden generation' players were finally coming good and gelling as a unit at international level. But it was, without doubt, the final chance at this level for many of those players. The golden generation were not youngsters any more. In fact, with the notable exception of players like Rooney and Walcott, the England starting eleven for most of the matches so far had been amongst the oldest in the tournament.

But they were standing up well to the rigours of the gruelling competition and many neutrals were tipping them to win.

Spain still had a lot to say about that.

In the minutes before kick-off, family and friends of Santiago Muñez were preparing for the match in their own particular way.

In Los Angeles, his grandmother, Mercedes, and his brother, Julio, were sitting in front of the television in their living room with a whole host of friends and neighbours. Mercedes was sitting in the same chair that she always sat in, wearing the same dress that she always wore for Santi's television appearances. She was quieter than usual, less ready with her predictions and forecasts. She was nervous.

In England, Jamie Drew was also nervous. He wanted Santi to play brilliantly, possibly even to score. But Jamie, as an Englishman, wanted England to emerge ultimately triumphant. And Jamie was also thinking that maybe, if things had worked out differently, he just might have been there, lining up to face his great friend on the opposite side of the pitch.

A few streets away, Roz's mum, Carol, had the television tuned in for the match as she played with little Rosie and pointed out Santi every time he appeared on screen during the warm-up. Carol was nervous too.

In Madrid, the bar run by Santi's mother, Rosa-Maria, and her husband, Miguel, was packed to the rafters with noisy, Spanish supporters, drinking and shouting and singing the praises of their team. Rosa-Maria was very nervous and every so often, as he filled a glass or listened to a shouted order, Miguel would give her a reassuring wink or a nod and a smile up at the television screen to suggest that all would be well.

In the stadium, Roz and Enrique were both feeling almost sick with nerves. Enrique had told Roz that today she was honorary Spanish rather than English, and today Roz wasn't arguing. But in the final countdown to the kick-off, which was rapidly approaching but seemed to be taking hours, they were both so nervous they couldn't speak.

And up in his television studio position, Gavin Harris was nervous, for his friend and for his country, although Gavin, as always, was talking nineteen to the dozen as he and other experts gave their thoughts on what lay ahead over the next ninety minutes – or more.

Out on the pitch, Santiago was also nervous, but his nerves were under control. Sometimes players just know that this is their day, their match, and as the whistle sounded for the kick-off and the crowd roared, Santiago sensed, like never before, that this *was* his day.

* * *

'Muñez is playing the game of his life,' said Gavin Harris. 'I've known him and played alongside him for years and he's always been up there with the best, but this . . . this is something else.'

There were nods of agreement from the other experts on the sofa. 'Brilliant,' said one. 'Totally dominant,' said another. 'Giving the English defence nightmares.'

The presenter listened in his earphone to instructions from his programme director before picking up the conversation with his studio guests. 'Let's take another look at the goal. Gavin, talk us through it.'

Everyone in the room and millions of viewers watched as Gavin described the action. 'We can see Muñez there in his own half when he first gets the ball. See how he has time to look up and decide on the best ball before he moves it thirty yards for Fàbregas to run on to. But watch him moving there, the intelligent run, looking for space and drawing two defenders with him. The English defence were panicking every time he got the ball by this stage. Now, when Torres collects from Xabi Alonso, there, you can see Muñez taking up the perfect position. And there, he receives the ball, and what a strike. *Fantastic* goal.'

The presenter nodded. 'So what do England do to counter this Muñez threat?'

Gavin smiled. 'If I knew the answer to that one, I'd be the England manager rather than Mr Capello. I guess England have got to hope that Santi can't keep up this level of performance in the second half.'

He could. He was inspired and inspirational to his team-mates as they dominated the second period. But although Spain went close, with Santi almost grabbing a second, there were no further goals until ten minutes before full time.

And then England scored.

It was against the run of play, but a fine goal for all that. Joe Cole collected out wide, carried the ball on and when he saw the cross wasn't on, laid it back into the path of the onrushing Steven Gerrard. He swung over a cross that was curling away from the keeper as it went into the box.

Rio Ferdinand, up from defence, came charging in and met the ball with a terrific header that went in the top corner.

England were back in it.

In Los Angeles, Mercedes thumped the arm of her chair in frustration. In England, Jamie leaped off his chair in delight. Up in the stands, Roz and Enrique shrieked with disappointment, and in the English television studios, Gavin and his colleagues yelled their joy.

'It could be extra time,' yelled the match commentator.

'I've got a feeling that's exactly what we'll get,' said Gavin.

And he was right again.

Forty

Some players were drinking from water bottles, others were lying on the pitch having tired legs pulled and stretched as the first signs of the dreaded cramp began to tighten weary muscles.

Coaches were barking out words of encouragement, both managers were giving orders and players were discussing quietly with one another what had gone badly and what had gone well and where they might snatch the victory.

Gavin Harris, in his television role, still had plenty to say. 'It's been a fantastic match, and Muñez has certainly been the man of the ninety minutes. But it's not over, far from it, and if anything England looked stronger in the last twenty minutes. And look at them out on the pitch now.'

The television cameras zoomed in on both sets of players as they took up their positions.

'Look at the way John Terry and Rio Ferdinand are urging the other players on. Stevie Gerrard too. They want this.'

They did. All the English players wanted it. But the Spanish wanted it just as much, and no one more so than Santiago Muñez.

And if an English victory was the drama that most were expecting to unfold over the next thirty minutes, then Santiago Muñez hadn't read the script.

He was everywhere; probing, darting, shooting, inspiring everyone in a red shirt to follow his example. And they were.

But legs were growing leaden all over the pitch; cramp was biting at screaming muscles. The first period ended, both managers by now having made all three of their permitted substitutions, partly with thoughts of a penalty shoot-out in their minds.

But a match isn't over until the final whistle sounds.

'It's Muñez again,' said the television commentator. 'I don't know where he's dragging these supplies of energy from, but he's looking so dangerous. Torres takes it on, to Villa, back to Torres again, and . . . *Muñez! Muñez has scored again! Spain are in front for a second time!*'

Down on the pitch, Santi went on a mazy run of celebration, which only stopped when first one, and then at least five more, of his teammates caught him and eventually dragged him to the ground before piling in on top of the ecstatic goal-scorer.

There were ten minutes remaining and Spain understandably took as long as the referee would permit to enjoy their goal celebrations.

But even then that mood of celebration didn't last for long.

Gerrard, unwilling to submit or to admit defeat, drove his tired legs on, and as the Spanish defence moved out he fed Lampard, who slipped the ball to Wayne Rooney, who clinically brought England back to all square for a second time.

Now England celebrated, and as the ref ordered them back for the restart, the Spanish players were urging each other on to one final effort.

Santi needed no urging; he could feel the thoughts of his family and friends willing him on as he went in search of the winner.

Collecting a throw out from Casillas he streaked away towards goal.

'He's looking for the hat-trick,' yelled the commentator.

'You're right, he is!' shouted Gavin, feeling a surge of excitement despite his loyalty to the English cause. 'He is!'

'Muñez now, moving at real pace,' said commentator. 'English defenders are closing in, but he's still going. Look at the way he avoided that tackle. And now he's . . . oh, and a wonderful, sliding challenge from Rio Ferdinand sends the ball out for a throw in.'

Ferdinand got to his feet and started to trot away, but Santi didn't get up.

'He's fallen awkwardly,' said Gavin Harris quickly. 'Look, Muñez is holding his right foot, he's not getting up. Surely it isn't the metatarsal again, that would be too cruel.'

Up in their seats, Roz and Enrique were on their feet; in Los Angeles, Mercedes's knuckles whitened as she gripped the arms of her chair; in England, Carol stopped playing with Rosie and stared at the screen; and at his home, Jamie sat on the edge of the sofa, whispering, 'Don't be hurt, Santi, don't be hurt.'

The challenge had been perfectly fair and Rio Ferdinand was the first to go back to ask Santi if he was OK. The awkward fall had caused his foot to twist as he went down, but he had to get up. He had to go on, there were no further substitutions available and there were still a few minutes to play. He was helped to his feet by the Spanish physio and by David Villa. Cheers and applause rang down from every side of stadium as Santi flexed his foot for a few moments and then slowly trotted away.

The match resumed and Santi cautiously but delightedly ran off the pain. The foot was fine; the metatarsal had come through the sternest of challenges.

Then, at last, the final whistle sounded.

'Penalties!' yelled Gavin Harris. 'And judging by their record in previous tournaments, that's the last thing England wanted.'

Both managers had handed over the lists of the first five nominated penalty takers for their teams.

The two keepers had shaken hands and embraced, both knowing that one of them was likely to be a national hero within the next few minutes.

On both sides players had stepped forward to offer their services as penalty takers. Some did the job for their clubs so were obvious choices. Others – those who felt they were up to the mental challenge of such an intimidating situation – also volunteered. All of them knew that the penalty they were about to take would be like none they had ever taken before.

Santi was a regular penalty taker and he wanted to take the first one for Spain now. 'Get us off to a good start,' he said to the manager.

'No,' the manager said, 'we'll save you for the

fifth. Maybe we'll have won it by then, England don't like penalties. But if we still need a winner, then you'll score for us.'

The players were moving forward to the centre circles and the two keepers were ready.

England had won the toss and would take the first kick. The senior players, the 'golden generation', were standing up, ready to be counted.

'*Yes!*' shouted Gavin Harris as Steven Gerrard sent the first penalty hard into the top corner of the net. 'That's the way to hit them; hard and fast and just out of the keeper's reach, even if he does dive the right way. Perfect.'

Fernando Torres walked past his Liverpool club-mate without even exchanging a look as he moved up to take the first Spanish penalty. It was just as good, following Gerrard's into almost exactly the same part of the net.

Frank Lampard was next. He buried the ball low down in the opposite corner and turned away, clenching his fist and grimacing with determination.

David Villa also hit the back of the net with a powerful, uncompromising drive.

Wayne Rooney stepped up. He looked tense – who wouldn't look tense in this situation? He placed the ball, moved back slowly, ran three steps forward . . . and slotted the ball home.

'This is good,' said Gavin in the studio. 'Neither keeper's got near to one so far.'

Cesc Fàbregas kept up the one hundred per cent record with a more delicate spot kick, placed rather than struck. But it was just as effective and counted just as much.

The two groups of players stood in the middle, arms over shoulders, willing each of their team-mates to succeed, knowing that someone must eventually fail, praying that it wouldn't be them.

Joe Cole placed the ball for the fourth English attempt. He struck it well, but Casillas had guessed the right way and his outstretched fingers made contact with the ball. For a split second the English fans' hearts were in their mouths. But then an audible, collective sigh of relief swept down from the stands as the partly parried ball continued over the line.

Xabi Alonso stepped up for Spain. His attempt struck the inside of the upright but went in.

'I've never seen such consistently brilliant penalties,' said Gavin Harris. 'This is unbelievable drama.'

John Terry was walking forward, and the vision of his missed spot kick, which cost Chelsea the 2008 Champions League final to Manchester United, was in millions of minds around the globe.

'Terry's looking to exorcise a few demons here,' said Gavin. 'Good luck to him. He's a brave man to even take it on.'

Terry strode forward like a giant. If there was any doubt in his mind it didn't show. He placed the ball, stood looking at it for a few seconds and then moved back and looked at the ball again. Who could know if the 2008 miss was lurking somewhere in the back of his mind as he ran forward? He struck the ball and again Casillas guessed the right way. But this time he didn't get near. Terry's penalty hit the back of the net and the big man stood gazing up at the heavens, looking as though he was offering up silent words of thanks.

It was down to Santiago Muñez to take the

fifth Spanish attempt. And now, with every one of the English penalties having counted, Santi could not afford to miss. If he did, Spain were out.

In the stadium, Roz couldn't look; she was gripping Enrique's hand so hard it was hurting. But he didn't pull it away. In Los Angeles, Mercedes stared, stone-faced at the television screen, not looking away for a second.

In England, Carol was standing behind the living-room door. Just like her daughter, she couldn't bear to look. Nearby, Jamie wanted England to win but he desperately did not want Santi to miss.

And neither did Gavin Harris. 'Almost unfair pressure on Santiago Muñez now as he stands ready to take the kick. He's been the player of the match, it would be unbearably cruel if he missed this one.'

Santi had rehearsed the kick in his mind at least five times. He knew exactly where the ball was going. He placed it carefully and deliberately, running the kick through in his mind yet again as he stepped back. He was ready.

He looked at the ball and then at the goal and then at the ball again. He didn't make eye contact with the keeper, the keeper wasn't in his thoughts, just the ball striking the back of the next.

He started to run. One, two, three strides and his right foot swung through with perfect timing and struck the ball sweetly. It flew away like a rocket. Santi couldn't have hit the shot any better; it was heading for the top right corner, exactly where it was meant to go.

And then somehow, miraculously, the keeper came flying across the goal, left arm outstretched, fingers magically seeking out and reaching the ball, like a magnet drawn to metal. The ball was pushed away with fingertips, bouncing out to safety. One half of the crowd roared with joy and the other groaned in misery.

It was an incredible save – a worthy winner of any penalty shoot-out – but Santi could hardly believe it.

He fell back on the ground as he heard the English players shouting their joy and delight, screaming that they were through to the final.

Santi stared up at the sky, wishing the ground would open and swallow him. The dream was over. Spain were out.

Forty-one

Santi was feeling better now. Time was beginning to heal the wounds of World Cup defeat.

In the minutes after the saved penalty he was inconsolable. It didn't matter what his teammates or the coaches said, it didn't matter that his two goals had taken Spain to the penalty shoot-out, it didn't matter that he had been adjudged Man of the Match and was even in line for the Golden Boot for the tournament's top goal-scorer. Nothing mattered. Spain were out and it was down to him.

But then gradually, Santi began to realize that it wasn't as simple as that. The defeat had happened over the full course of the match; all the twists and turns and moments of drama had contributed to the way it had ended. One kick here, a tackle or a save there, and the match may have ended differently again. That was sport, that was football; that was what made it so exciting and thrilling for participants and supporters alike.

And England had been worthy winners. Now they were preparing to face Brazil in the final, after the South American team had snatched victory in the other semifinal with an extra time goal.

Everyone was supportive and no one laid any blame at Santi's feet. Mercedes called a couple of hours after the match and managed to offer her usual criticism, without even mentioning the saved penalty.

She praised the goals, the fantastic runs, the box-to-box effort, but remembered one incident when Santi should have passed instead of running with the ball.

'You should have laid the ball off,' she grumbled in her usual way. 'There was a good pass on.'

It made Santi smile for the first time since the match ended. And when Mercedes added that she loved him and was proud of him and that his father would have been proud of him if he had lived to see the game, it brought a lump to Santi's throat.

Gavin called, Jamie called, Carol sent a photo of a smiling Rosie to his phone; Enrique had sent a text before he'd even left the stadium, saying simply, 'You're the best.'

And when Roz saw him she simply hugged him and told him that she loved him.

Everyone was there for him, and not just his family and friends. People he'd never even met were writing, sending letters to newspapers and posting messages of support on Internet chat sites.

And the passing of time, just a few days, was helping. He wasn't dreaming about the penalty miss every time he went to sleep now.

He felt better, a lot better.

Now it was the day of the World Cup Final – the climax of the world's greatest football tournament – and Santi and Enrique were sitting together in Santi's hotel room, ready to watch it on television. Spain had won the third place play-off the day before, beating Germany by a goal to nil, with David Villa scoring. Santi had his medal, his permanent memento of the most incredible tournament.

The television was on and Santi and Enrique watched as the teams stood proudly singing their national anthems. Back in England, Santi knew that streets would be deserted – a nation was waiting to cheer on their heroes. Waiting to lift the ultimate trophy for the first time since 1966. As the players trotted away to prepare for the kick-off, the voice of Gavin Harris spoke excitedly about the match to come.

Football was moving on, it already had moved on. That was what made it so exciting.

Santi smiled. 'I watched the final four years ago and I could never have imagined what would happen this time around. It's been amazing. I'll never forget it.'

'And maybe in four more years you'll make it to the final,' said Enrique.

'Maybe,' said Santi laughing. 'Or maybe by then it will be your turn. Who knows?'

And then the whistle sounded and the World Cup Final was underway . . .

GOAL!

The official tie-in novelization by Robert Rigby

One word unites the world . . .

GOAL!

Santiago – a young Latino in Los Angeles – has only one dream in life: to play football. Offered a trial at one of England's top Premiership clubs, he flies halfway across the world to give it his best shot. He has skill, flair and determination. But has he the pace and stamina he will need for the English game?

A gripping tale of trial and tribulation, tragedy and triumph, set against the backdrop of the world's most popular and exciting sport.

ISBN 978 0552 554039

www.rbooks.co.uk

GOAL II

LIVING THE DREAM

The official tie-in novelization by Robert Rigby

THEY'RE THE BIGGEST FOOTBALL CLUB
ON THE PLANET.

THEY DEMAND TOTAL DEDICATION

100% COMMITMENT.

AND THEY WANT SANTI . . .

When Santiago Munez signs to Real Madrid, he is determined to win a regular first-team place alongside Beckham, Raul, Ronaldo and the other galacticos. But the pressure is on as Real Madrid play vital games in the Champions League – aiming for the greatest trophy in European club football . . .

A riveting tale of talent and opportunity, set against the backdrop of the world's most beautiful game.

THIS TIME THE DREAM IS REAL!

ISBN 978 0552 554084

www.rbooks.co.uk